"I'm no... ...body to exercise the horse for an hour a day."

Cadence took a deep breath and continued. "I'm looking for somebody to ride him. Full-time. To jump him in competitions."

Dace stared at her with open astonishment. "Me? I'm just a cowboy."

"I know you are. I'm talking about what you could be."

He gave her a hard smile. "I like what I am right now."

She was so frustrated, she said, "I'll pay you double whatever you're making." She knew it was completely the wrong tack to take, but she didn't know what else to do.

"I'm not for sale," he replied tersely. "I'm not interested in your money. I'm not interested in your fancy-pants riding. And I most definitely am not interested in working for you."

"I could have you fired," she threatened.

"Yes, ma'am, you could," he agreed, then walked out the door.

Quinn Wilder, a Canadian writer, was born and raised in Calgary, but now lives in the Okanagan Valley away from the bustle of a city. She has had a variety of jobs, but her favorite pastime has always been writing. She graduated from the Southern Alberta Institute of Technology Journalism Arts program in 1979. Since then, she has free-lanced, and her list of credits includes magazine articles, educational material, scripts, speeches and so on. Her first novel became a Harlequin, marking a high point in her career. She enjoys skiing and horseback riding.

Books by Quinn Wilder

HARLEQUIN ROMANCE
2772—THAT MAN FROM TEXAS
2886—TO TAME A WILD HEART
2904—DAUGHTER OF THE STARS
3096—HIGH HEAVEN
3191—OUTLAW HEART

RIDE A STORM
Quinn Wilder

Harlequin Books

TORONTO • NEW YORK • LONDON
AMSTERDAM • PARIS • SYDNEY • HAMBURG
STOCKHOLM • ATHENS • TOKYO • MILAN
MADRID • WARSAW • BUDAPEST • AUCKLAND

Original hardcover edition published in 1991
by Mills & Boon Limited

ISBN 0-373-03258-7

Harlequin Romance first edition March 1993

RIDE A STORM

CHAPTER ONE

"DAMNED COWBOY."

Cadence Copperthorne was angry. Furiously, savagely, dangerously angry. She slammed her car door so hard that the windshield rattled. Then she paused, and glared up the wide, long, paved path that led to the sprawling mansion that was home.

She pictured herself striding up the walk, her fury unmistakable in her every step. She wanted to take the four marble steps two at a time, cross the wide veranda in one angry stride, have the satisfaction of seeing servants scurrying out of her way...

"Damned cowboy," she muttered again, unwilling to let her anger become defused by the effort it was going to cost her to get up the path and then up the stairs that led to the front entrance of the pillared plantation-style monstrosity that was home.

Panting slightly, a few moments later, she paused in the shadow of the veranda. For a moment she gazed off into the distance. The sky was intensely blue, and cloudless. The countryside was still the vibrant green of the first fresh days of summer. The leaves on the massive maples around the house whispered against each other in the peaceful stillness. The lush Southern Alberta hills rolled gently toward the smoky blue of the distant foothills, the towering Rockies.

For an unguarded moment, the tranquillity of the scene nibbled tentatively at Cadence, some memory of contentment calling to her. But it was

followed relentlessly by a more precise memory of
the long hay-scented days of summers past, of hard,
satisfying work, of her horses.

She turned her head and her gaze moved, against
her will, to the area to the side of the house. The
white-fenced riding school was empty. The practice
jumps had been put away. She could just see a
corner of the stable, gray with white trim. It seemed
oddly ghostly and silent in the summer sun, though
she knew her horses were in there.

Not Storm, though. He must be in the paddock
on the other side of the stable. If he was in a box
stall, she would hear him, restless, snorting. A pain,
so strong it seemed physical, twisted at her heart,
but she brushed the feeling savagely away. She had
other things to deal with! Her anger was giving her
blessed respite from her hurt, and she planned to
use that to full advantage.

She swung her eyes abruptly away from the riding
school, and looked west, toward another world,
shamelessly stoking the angry fire within her. Her
eyes narrowed on the barns, which formed the
border of the ranch side of this huge holding of
her father's.

Two worlds gently coexisted on one gigantic
property. The house, her stables and riding area,
the pool, the formal gardens made up one world.
One of refinement and elegance. And not a stone's
throw away was the other world. Located far
enough away that the smells and dust couldn't
offend the senses of those in "the castle," as this
monstrosity of a house was affectionately referred
to by the locals. And close enough that her father
still felt he had a hand in running the place, which
was something of a laugh.

The seemingly odd combination coexisted harmoniously. Cadence had always liked the sight of the barns. There was energy down there; dust rising; the timbre of masculine voices raised above the sounds of cattle and horses. There was a raw beauty in the pure physical strength and stamina that was required of the men who worked the ranch part of her home.

"Stupid, ignorant cowboy," she muttered, eyeing the distant red of the barns. Voicing the words gave her a satisfying surge of energy. She stamped across the last stretch of porch, went in the door and slammed it so hard that the beveled glass rattled in its frame.

"Timothy!" she yelled. She moved gracelessly across the wide entrance hall and went through the french-pane doors and into the book-lined sitting room next to it. "Timothy!"

She eased onto a dainty silk-covered antique sofa. Her need to be careful with her hip, injured four months ago in a riding accident, thwarted her need to be aggressive. She made up for it by throwing the hated cane halfway across the polished mahogany floors. Now *there* was a noise that satisfied her!

Timothy was in the doorway, and had witnessed the action. Good, she thought. He would know she was not to be trifled with, and certainly not to be pitied. His face was impassive. She saved him the awkwardness of a greeting.

"Get me the barns on the phone."

"Barns?" he asked, his voice smooth and calming and professional.

"The cattle portion of Mr. Copperthorne's empire," she replied coolly. She had grown up with this man overseeing the needs of this rather ridiculous house. He was not an employee. He was family. And if she let down her guard for a minute his sympathy would ooze all over her, robbing her of her pride.

In a small book-lined alcove to one side of a grossly formal fireplace, a paper rustled. She glanced over, to see her father peering a trifle timidly at her over the top of the paper.

His look satisfied her. At least it was obvious she was angry. Maybe that would give her a break from the painful caring in his eyes, the sadness.

"Is there a problem at the barns, Cadence?"

She went rigid. "Don't call me that, please."

"We're all trying to remember you prefer Cade now. However, you must make allowances. Timothy and I have been calling you Cadence for twenty-two years."

She closed her eyes against him. Against his hurt. Against his pleading. His eyes always seemed to beg her, Be what you were—Cadence. The name said it all: a young woman who had moved with the strength and grace of a top athlete. A young woman whose soul had danced to the energetic tattoo of her dreams.

She opened her eyes, only to look directly into the photographic portrait he refused to take down from the mantel. It had been taken very shortly after a winning ride, and it had captured the Cadence she had used to be. She was in her riding habit, the black velvet of her jacket making her hair seem like flame—dancing, untamed waves of orange and gold and red. The only thing she had ever detested about her sport was that she had had to tame her hair.

It had become her trademark that, after a victory, she pulled off her helmet and impatiently yanked the ribbon from her hair, giving her head a shake so that her wild mane sprang free. The photographer had captured that moment, captured the lingering laughter and excitement in her eyes... captured her cadence.

Cadence. Yes, once it had been her name, and she had loved having a name like that. Loved the ring of it over the raspy old loudspeakers of a thousand riding arenas. "And now we have Cadence Copperthorne riding..."

Now, the name only mocked her. She had shortened it, first to Cay, but, finding that too plain, she had finally settled on Cade.

"Is something wrong at the barns?" her father repeated.

Timothy slipped in with the phone. "I have Mr. Jones on the line. He's the foreman——"

She snatched the phone. "Sloan? It's... Miss Copperthorne here." Out of the corner of her eye she saw the surprise register in both Timothy's and her father's eyes. Okay, she wasn't always that certain what to call herself any more, either. But Sloan wouldn't know who Cade was, and she couldn't introduce herself as Cadence after she'd just dressed her father down for calling her that.

Besides, it wouldn't hurt the old cowpoke to realize she'd grown up. She was no longer the little girl who sneaked down to his barns, who'd been the recipient of his gentle gifts... sleigh rides for her and her friends on crisp winter nights, a beautiful white kitten with six toes—"the Finns say they're lucky, miss." He was the man who'd teased her gently when she'd taken up her "fancy-pants" riding, and yet often come up to the fresh white-painted paddocks, so different from his own worn and wired-together corrals, to watch her. He'd even told her once she had a damned fine way with a horse. It was about as high a compliment as he gave.

But he was just one more person on a long list of people who belonged to the past now, who belonged to Cadence, a Cadence who was no more.

"There's a cowhand headed in from the west section. Is he there yet?"

"No," and then a slight hesitation. "Ma'am."

Sloan had always called her Princess. She had wanted him to realize she was grown up, but now she was a little sorry that he had. Well, he'd probably be just like Timothy, if she gave him the opening, oozing unwanted sympathy all over her.

"He should be there any minute. When he gets in, you tell him I want to see him at the house. Pronto."

His hesitation was loaded with unvoiced questions. Once he would have asked them. Now he just said, "Yes, ma'am," and hung up.

She slammed the receiver back onto the phone, and looked out of the window, fuming.

"Is there a problem—er—Cade?" her father asked.

The way he said it, heavy with reproach, was almost worse than being called Cadence. Almost. Not quite.

"I don't have a problem. There's a cowboy out there riding for home who has a few seconds more to be blissfully unaware that *he* has a problem."

"Who is it?"

She frowned. Once, she had recognized everyone who worked on her father's distinctly divided property, from gardeners to cowboys. She had known everyone's names. But that was a long time ago. Before she had become so totally engrossed in the pursuit of her own dreams.

"I don't know. He was quite a distance away, but I'm pretty sure it was nobody I've ever seen before."

Pretty sure? Now that was an out-and-out lie. She had been driving, recklessly fast, home from a session of physiotherapy. Out of the corner of her eye she had seen him, slammed on the brakes, and got out of the car. Leaning her weight on the hood she had watched him, transfixed.

The man and horse had been far enough away that they would probably not even notice her, this arresting pair, the black horse going flat out, the lean rider who sat him with such incredible confidence. It seemed, somehow, that she had been transported into an earlier age. An age of hard men and hard horses, an age of sweat and leather, an age where men were born to horses and saddles, and celebrated the freedom of their lives just like this—by racing the wind across an undulating, unbroken sea of green grass. His ruggedness and his freedom had communicated across the distance, and had arrested her. She had appreciated the scene with her whole heart and soul, had become totally absorbed in a moment of untamed magnificence.

And then the illusion of an endless sea of green grass, of an earlier, wilder, freer time, had been shattered. The horse and rider had been approaching a fence. He would, she'd known, become an ordinary man in an ordinary time, tamed, confined by an ordinary fence. She had started to turn away, not wanting to see that transformation.

Wanting, instead, to keep the picture of him, untamed, in her mind. Not wanting to see him do something as mundane as slow his horse and get off, and open the gate in the fence and lead his horse through and get back on.

She had been lowering herself back into the driver's seat of her car when, out of the corner of her eye, she'd noticed that he was not slowing down. Utter disbelief had seemed to stop her heart. She'd levered herself back out of the car and stared at him with horror. He couldn't possibly be planning to take that fence. Not at that speed. Not on a stocky little cow horse. Not with a stock saddle.

And then, impossibly, he'd been sailing. Up and up, frozen for that exhilarating second at the top of the jump and then going down. He hadn't missed a stride, and he hadn't looked backward at the fence he had just conquered with such total assurance.

In a way, it was the sheer beauty of it that had made her so angry. Not the fact that he'd been reckless, but the fact that he'd been reckless with a confidence that had crossed the distance and touched her like a physical touch. He had never slowed down. Not before the fence and not after it. He didn't even know what he had. He didn't know it was a gift to be able to leave the bonds of earth, even for a few split seconds.

What had stirred in her was a rage of envy that he had something that she had lost.

"What exactly did he do?"

Her voice crackled with indignation as she answered her father's question. "He jumped a stupid little fence, and he did it with a stupid little cow pony in a stupid big stock saddle."

She was aware that she actually hated this man whom she had caught such a brief and golden glance of. Damn it all, she did not want to be reminded that such effortless grace still existed in this world. He was soaring with eagles, while she was earthbound, a captive of her broken wings.

"What exactly do you plan to say to him?"

"I plan to tell him he should be shot for riding a horse that doesn't belong to him so recklessly. I may fire him."

She looked warningly at her father, who looked as if he might be about to mention that firing cowboys was not exactly in her jurisdiction.

"Well, if it's all the same to you, perhaps I'll just leave you to it." Her father gathered up his paper nervously and left the room. He could not bear confrontation. She knew the whole community speculated on how such a meek and mild man had survived her firebrand mother, and now herself.

Behind the door, she was irritated to hear her father and Timothy exchanging remarks about her.

"Did you see her eyes, man?" she heard her father reply to something Timothy had said that she hadn't quite caught. "She lives!"

"So I saw, sir," came the muffled reply, and she could hear a contented note in it.

She groaned with frustration. This was exactly the type of thing she hated about having a handicap. Nobody took a rage seriously.

Or maybe, she considered slowly, it had just been so long since she had had one of her rather famous fits of temper that they took it as a sign they were getting her back after all. Lord almighty, she wished they would let Cadence die in peace.

Still, throwing a regretful look at where she had thrown the cane, she managed to get herself up and used the furniture to move around to the mirror.

There was a sparkle in her brown, gold-flecked eyes that hadn't been there for a long time. And banners of good healthy *angry* color had chased that invalid pallor from her cheeks.

"Unfortunately, I think I am going to live," she admitted to the mirror. She inspected herself slowly. She *was* looking much better. The dark circles of pain were gone from underneath her eyes, the gauntness was disappearing from her cheeks.

In fact ... She stepped back from the mirror and squinted hard at herself. Her tough training had always made her lithe and muscular. She had rarely carried more than a hundred and ten pounds on her five-foot-seven frame. But the weeks of inactivity were showing.

She actually looked vaguely curvaceous. "Good Lord, Cade," she muttered to herself, "are you running to fat?"

Too late, she realized that her reflection had been joined by another one. He had entered the room silently and stood just inside the door, his eyes meeting hers in the mirror. Though his eyes were shadowed by the brim of a Stetson, they were unmistakably and astonishingly indigo.

"Well, certainly not from this angle," he drawled with dry appreciation, his eyes flicking insolently to her *derrière*, and then coming to rest, expressionless, back on the reflection of her face.

He took off the cowboy hat, ran a hand through a tangle of dark curls. "Afternoon, ma'am."

His voice was as soft and sensuous as velvet being rubbed along the back of her neck. There was a faint drawl around the edges of his words, but no nasal rawness. His tone was deep and smooth—so there was no reason at all for the sound of it to make her nearly jump out of her skin. The start sent a piercing shaft of pain through her hip.

She turned with slow dignity, her eyebrows arched coldly at the intruder, her pert nose tilted a little higher than normal to cover her pain and her awkwardness. She had planned to be sitting for this interview. Now she was going to be forced to stand—or give a demonstration of how she hobbled around the furniture like an eighty-year-old grandmother. Dammit! How could she allow herself to get caught like this?

"How did you get in here?" she snapped, hating him for wrecking the cool scenario she had planned for dressing him down. "How dare you act like a ... a Peeping Tom?"

A thick black eyebrow arched upward. "The door was open ... ma'am. I knocked, but——" He shrugged with a certain arrogance, as if he had better things to do than wait around for doors to be opened for him. "Had I known you were deep in conversation with yourself, I wouldn't have interrupted. As it was, I thought you were asking my opinion."

She knew he had thought no such thing. Imagine the nerve of him, spying on her, and then turning it around so that she looked like Narcissus.

"Well, I wasn't asking your opinion," she snapped. It was now apparent to her that nothing was going to go according to her plan. This was no meek, humble cowboy who was going to let her vent her temper on him. Who was going to stammer an apology, agree never to jump the cow horses

again, and then run for his life back to the safety
of his cattle.

He was a big, hard man, with whipcord muscles,
a stern, impassive face that tended toward dangerous because of the unconscious glitter of sensuality
in his eyes. She severely doubted that he was going
to be intimidated by her—and was rather annoyed
to discover she was somewhat intimidated by the
sheer rugged masculinity of him.

He had obviously ducked his head under a tap
before he ventured up to the big house. His black
hair, too long, and yet attractively roguish, curled
damply around his ears. The hollows of his cheeks,
the square of his jaw, were faintly whisker-
shadowed—one of those men who would have to
shave twice a day if he were in a more civilized line
of work. But his work, and the physical toll of his
work, were stamped on to his face—his nose had
the sudden jut of a break, and a thin scar divided
one of his dark, wickedly arching eyebrows in half.
The weathered bronze of his skin made the hue of
his eyes seem hauntingly deep, the color of a
summer midnight, a blue that ranged somewhere
between purple and black.

He radiated a casual and sure strength, something of the cattle he'd wrestled and the horses he'd
broken carried within him, as well as showing in
the depth of his chest, the knotted muscle in the
long length of sun-browned arms visible below the
rolled sleeves of a denim shirt faded nearly white.
His legs were incredibly long and lean, molded by
Levi's nearly as faded as the shirt.

"Ma'am?"

She shook her head slightly, trying to remember
why they were here. He was a devastatingly at-

tractive man. She recognized her appreciation of
that fact as being purely clinical, and yet, absurdly,
she looked for an answering appreciation in the astounding depths of those eyes. Despite his earlier
and altogether too intimate comment, not a flicker
of interest disturbed that flatly impassive surface.

Once, she had enjoyed the fact that men seemed
to find her almost irresistibly attractive. Now their
interest tended to last until precisely the moment
they saw her move.

She decided, peevishly or vainly, not to move
until she had finished conducting this interview,
even though it pained her to stand for too long,
and particularly when she was standing so stiffly
upright so as not to give away even a hint of her
handicap.

And then he destroyed it all by glancing at the
cane on the floor in front of him, bending over
easily to retrieve it, and moving toward her, his expression unchanged.

"Would you like this?"

She snatched it from him, and thumped it into
the floor close enough to his toe that he had to pull
back to avoid getting stamped on. She noticed the
narrowing of his eyes, the tiny sparks of danger
that flitted through those placid indigo pools.

She sank back onto the sofa. She did not offer
him a seat, though he did not seem particularly offended. He also did not seem particularly intimidated by her summons, which annoyed her.

"I'm Dace Stanton," he finally said, his voice
calm, and sure, but indicating that he wanted to
get down to business and be on his way.

Obviously, he didn't find her even remotely attractive. She wondered if it was the cane that al-

lowed him to dismiss her so readily. Or maybe he was married. Her gaze flicked quickly to his un-adorned ring finger, and then she reddened when she saw that those alert eyes had not missed the fact, though it brought no change to his expression.

She decided she disliked Dace Stanton for reasons other than that he had made her angry by jumping a horse he had no right to be jumping. Twice, in the space of a very few minutes, he had managed to remind her of something she was putting the entire force of her will into forgetting. Limitations.

Once, this might have been the kind of man she would have, almost playfully, tested her charms on. There had been quite a few men whom she had wooed and won just for the fun of it. Of course, she had had to get rid of them when they started getting jealous of her dream. And they always did, because her dream had demanded everything, an almost impossible single-mindedness of purpose.

Lionel had been the only man who shared her zeal. Their understanding of the price of their dreams had gone a long way in making their re-lationship seem so strong. Or rather, she corrected herself, giving it the illusion of strength. Once the chips were down ...

She sniffed and raised her chin a notch. She did not return the courtesy of introducing herself to Dace Stanton. She squinted narrowly at him, hoping to make him uncomfortable. The man looked totally at ease, resting his weight on one hip, eyeing her sardonically. Once he shifted his black cowboy hat from one hand to another, though the gesture wasn't nervous at all. It made him look en-tirely at home; she almost expected he might start whistling, he seemed so totally at ease and unintimidated both by the richness of his surroundings and the barely contained bristling of the head honcho's daughter.

His eyes flicked around the room with casual interest, and then strayed to the view. Finally he looked back at her. He ran a strong hand through the dark, drying silk of his hair, and cocked his head at her.

"The boss said you wanted to see me...ma'am."

"I'm the boss," she informed him coldly.

His features had been impassive. Now they became icily remote. A hood fell smoothly over his eyes, darkening them to a shade that approached pitch. He shifted his weight, but not with discomfort. A certain rigidity had entered the loose-limbed way he held himself. He nodded blandly at her, acknowledging the message, but a muscle flickering in the line of his jaw indicated that his temper was being carefully leashed.

"The way you treated that horse this afternoon was utterly irresponsible." Her voice was frozen, devoid of the shards of shattered dreams that being around this man had pushed uncomfortably into the forefront of her mind.

The flickering in his jaw stopped abruptly. His eyes narrowed incredulously on her. "I've never treated a horse irresponsibly in my life," he said tersely.

For a moment she was left wordless. He meant it. And his passion for horses was evident in each terse word. She had the uneasy notion his feeling for horses could easily match her own.

Then she had the uneasy feeling it would be dangerous to assume she had anything in common with this man. She glared defiantly at him. "The facts speak for themselves. What if he hadn't cleared that fence?''

The man was silent for an uncomfortably long time. Finally he spoke. ''Oh. That.'' His tone was dismissive.

''You could have killed that horse if you'd hit the——''

''I happen to know that particular fence could be knocked over by a feather,'' he cut her off. She caught an astounding note in the arrogant rasp of his voice. Sheepishness?

''Now how would you know that?''

He studied the well-worn pointed toe of his boot for a moment. ''The gate isn't fastened. And the top hinge is missing.''

She did not want to be cheated out of her angry speech, though undoubtedly a gate in that condition would go over at the rap of a feather, never mind a hoof. ''Well, if you're so familiar with the condition of that gate, isn't it your bloody job to fix it?''

He studied his other toe, thoughtfully. But, even though his head was ducked, she could see the tide of brick-red rising up the strong column of his throat.

''I took it apart in the first place.'' He raised his head abruptly. His chin rose proudly. The sheepishness was gone from his expression. It was proud and unapologetic. His eyes met hers unflinchingly.

''You practically dismantled the fence so that you could jump it?'' she asked in amazement. ''Why? Does that beat getting down and opening it? That takes laziness to new limits, doesn't it?''

His chin tilted at an even haughtier angle, a light that could only be called dangerous burned in the fathomless depths of his eyes.

"For one thing, I haven't dismounted from a horse to open a gate since I was three, and for another——"

She almost laughed aloud at his foolish cowboy pride coming first, though his eyes warned her it would be very foolish to laugh right now—boss or no.

"And, for another, no one has ever accused me of being lazy. I work hard, and I do my job well. You don't know a thing about me, lady. I apologize if my jumping the horse appeared foolhardy and reckless . . . from a distance. But that certainly doesn't give you the right to attack my character. Do you understand me?"

She watched him wide-eyed. He'd been a magnificent specimen before, but now he was incredible. For all that his tone had remained measured and infinitely reasonable, his eyes were sparking, his nose flaring. Cadence was stunned to find herself placed on the defensive, and she didn't like it one bit.

"I understand you," she informed him with icy hauteur, not allowing him to see for one minute that she'd been briefly intimidated by him. "However, it seems to me that the welfare of the cattle are your first responsibility and that they certainly could have pushed over that gate."

"Maybe," he said tautly, "but when was the last time you saw a cow in that particular field?"

She felt herself go crimson under his piercing gaze. "I don't generally concern myself with where the cattle are," she said snootily. Dammit, she realized he had her on the defensive again.

"And do you generally concern yourself with what the cowhands are doing?" he asked softly.

"If I feel an animal is being abused, I'm going to say something about it!"

"I told you I wasn't abusing the animal."

"Oh, good. I have your word on that."

"My word is worth a lot in this part of the country." His voice held a note of lethal softness. "Look, Miss Copperthorne, I appreciate your concern for the animal..."

His tone struck her as being mildly sarcastic.

"...but the situation was not as it appeared. I wasn't in any way being reckless. I was well aware of the animal's capabilities, and my own."

She was sure her mouth had dropped open at his tone. He was indicating that this interview was over! She snapped her mouth shut and glared at him.

"How on earth would you be aware of a cow horse's capabilities over a fence?"

He looked her directly in the eyes, his face absolutely devoid of apology. In fact, a wicked trace of humor seemed to be flickering deep beneath that sapphire surface of his eyes.

"I guess," he drawled, "it would be safe to assume I've jumped that particular pony before... ma'am."

"That is exactly my point," she gasped icily. "I do not consider it safe to be jumping cow horses. Neither you nor the horse had been trained for that activity."

He shrugged a large shoulder with a laziness that was given lie by the scathing intelligence of his eyes. "What are you really angry about?" he asked softly. "I jumped the horse. I admit it. It never occurred to me that I needed training to do it. I didn't break my neck, and I didn't come remotely close to injuring the horse. So what do you want from me?"

She had to bite her tongue to keep the furious flow of words back. She wanted to call him every name she could think of, and then fire him besides. It humiliated her that he knew the anger was about something else. But she didn't want to make a complete fool of herself by losing control—and she didn't want to fire him, either. She had a feeling he'd just shrug, pick up his saddle and be gone.

And there was one other reason to leash her temper. She had to know. She was burning to know.

So she looked away from him, fought her temper and finally looked back with something approaching composure.

"All I want to know is why," she finally managed to say huskily. "Did you go to all that trouble just to shave a few seconds off the ride in?"

He hesitated, his gaze thoughtful. Something in him seemed to relax, a touch of the wariness left his eyes. "No, ma'am."

"Then why?" she prodded.

He looked at her levelly. Shrugged. "I like it."

For a split second his guard was completely down, and she felt the shock of recognition tingle up her spine. That was what she'd recognized when he'd jumped. That was what had brought the tears pricking to her eyes, and the lump to her throat.

He'd understated it. He didn't just like it. He loved it. She had seen it in the smoothness of that jump, in the utter confidence his guidance had bestowed on that clumsy little cow horse. For a moment, she had glimpsed herself in a stranger pounding over a field and clearing a fence, in his passion for that fence and for the capabilities of the horse beneath him. She had felt the impact of it from half a mile away.

"You can go," she said tersely, not looking at him, staring down at the hands knotting and un-knotting in her lap.

He hesitated. She could feel his eyes resting on her. Then he spun on the heel of that well-worn cowboy boot and strode out of the room.

The room was tinged pink with the light of the setting sun when her father found her, sitting there, staring.

"Well, dear, did you accomplish what you set out to do?"

"Yes." It was true, though when she'd angrily called the barns earlier she had not even been aware herself what was really going on.

Dace Stanton was stronger than she. It was that simple. Her heart had recognized it as soon as she'd witnessed him and that fence. He was strong enough to complete the task that had been too big for her, that had destroyed her. Damn him to hell.

Her voice had a weary note in it when she addressed her father again.

"I found the man who can ride Storm Warrior."

CHAPTER TWO

DACE cursed soundly as the board splintered under the pressure of the screw. The wood of the gate was too rotten to take a new hinge. With silent temper he turned and hurled the hinge as far as he could, and then turned back to the gate. Bracing his one leg on the bottom bar, and one arm on the top one, he threw his weight behind the board, and the nails groaned until the piece of fence wrenched free. It gave him less satisfaction than he had hoped to break it over his knee—the wood was rotten and gave way easily, with a whisper rather than a snap.

"Hell," Dace snorted with disgust.

"Thinking of anyone in particular?"

Dace whirled in surprise. Sloan sat, not three yards from him, astride the big Appaloosa he favored.

Dace was pretty sure the man was part Indian. He could come up on a person with impossible quiet—and he could read minds. Because Dace *had* been thinking of someone in particular when he'd finally given in to the demands of his temper—not that he was going to admit that to Sloan.

Dace plucked his shirt off a fence post, wiped the sweat from his glistening arms and face, and then nodded at the partially dismantled gate.

"Wood's rotten. We'll have to put in a new one."

Sloan nodded, without a great deal of interest. "You been up to anything *else* I should know about?" he asked casually.

Dace shot Sloan a wary glance. He'd told Sloan about his meeting with Princess Copperthorne. He'd been pretty sure she was going to be talking to Sloan anyway, and he'd been prepared for his walking papers. But Sloan had only told him mildly to fix the gate and not jump the cow horses. If Cadence Copperthorne had talked to Sloan about the incident, he didn't mention it, and Dace grudgingly admitted to himself that she probably hadn't involved Sloan. Which for some reason didn't lessen the anger he felt when he thought about her one little bit. And he thought about that snooty red-headed witch more than he wanted to.

"I've been meaning to go into town and do some raping and pillaging," Dace said dryly, "but I've been working on this gate since dawn. Maybe on my coffee break, though."

Sloan chuckled amicably. "Sarcastic pup. Just wondered why she'd want to see you again, that's all."

Dace felt himself go rigid. He forced his muscles to relax under Sloan's interested gaze. "Does she?" he asked flatly.

"Asked me to tell you to go around to the big house around eleven. You got no idea what it's about?"

"No, sir."

Sloan was not in the least deterred by Dace's cool use of a formality to try and curb his friendly interest. "Guess she might want to have tea with you." He slapped his thigh happily at his humor.

Dace glared at him, and Sloan gazed down at him with wicked amusement.

"You ain't scared of her, are you, Dace?"

"Scared isn't exactly the right word," Dace muttered.

"She's a beautiful woman," Sloan noted casually.

Dace shrugged. "She might be—if she didn't look as if she'd been sucking lemons."

The friendliness left Sloan's face. "You might remember how bad she's been hurt."

"Plenty of people have been hurt," Dace came back quietly, "and they don't use it as an excuse to make everybody else in the world miserable along with them."

"I thought maybe you would see it weren't just her hip that got busted." Sloan was looking at him with disappointment. "It was her heart. Damn it, son, you should know about hurting hearts."

For a moment, Dace felt as if he had been slammed in the stomach. Yes, Lord, yes, he knew about hurting hearts.

But he wasn't sure Cadence Copperthorne possessed such a thing. He recalled her—that pinched face, the coldness in her eyes and tone, the utter arrogance of her. And all that combined with an unearthly beauty, flaming red hair and huge eyes. Brown, but so generously flecked with amber that he had come away with the impression that her eyes were gold. Lioness eyes. And that was how he had her pegged: a huntress. The type of woman—bad leg, or no—who brought men to their knees with total ease, and who enjoyed doing it besides.

"Everybody thought she'd marry her coach," Sloan offered offhandedly. "They were pretty much inseparable. He rode, too. He ain't been around much since the accident, though."

Personally, Dace was not sure he blamed the man, though it wouldn't do to tell Sloan that. Sloan felt a stubborn loyalty for his "Princess," and there wasn't going to be any arguing about it.

"I'll go see her at eleven," Dace said. He picked up the hammer and used the claw end of it to wrench another rotting board from the gate.

"If you headed back now, you could grab a shower first," Sloan hinted with a meaningful glance at his watch.

Dace turned and looked at him levelly, and then turned back to the gate.

He was aware he looked—and likely smelled— as if he'd been working. But dammit if he was going to let that redheaded vixen think he'd rush out and shave and shower just because of her royal summons. If he stayed as he was, she might get the message that he did not particularly appreciate being summoned at her whim.

Sloan was still sitting there, looking expectant. Dace flashed him a look.

"I'm not going courting," he said grimly. He was pretty sure he caught a faintly disappointed look before Sloan had the good sense to turn and ride away.

He was coming.

Cade stood at the window, watching the tall cowboy walk down the dusty road toward the house. She was surprised. Most cowboys needed their horses to look graceful and strong. Earthbound they were about as graceful as ducks wobbling out of water. But Dace Stanton walked with a powerful and ground-eating stride, his spine straight and his shoulders back, an innate pride and a subtle sensuality in his movement.

She felt a shiver of anxiety. Her father had introduced an element of doubt into her plans. He thought her plan was foolish. Even worse, he did not think Dace would do it.

Cade tossed her head at the figure walking down the road. Nonsense. She always got what she wanted.

An unwanted picture of Lionel crowded her brain. Okay—maybe not always. But her recent string of unfortunate events only made her all the more determined to have her way now.

Timothy came in. "Miss Copperthorne, Mr. Stanton is here to see you."

Timothy had recognized that innate dignity in Dace Stanton, too, she noted. He had introduced him as her equal.

She settled herself on the couch. She tucked the cane behind it, wanting nothing to suggest weakness to this man. She was rather surprised to find her heart hammering in her throat when Dace came into the room.

An aroma wafted in with him. The smell of soap and sunshine mingled enticingly with the scent of horses and sweat. The manliness of it contrasted sharply with the dainty refinement of this room. It made her extraordinarily aware of his masculinity, and her eyes strayed to the sun-browned muscles of his arms. She was shocked by the renegade feeling of yearning that blasted through her. The feeling tickled momentarily—and then cut with a razor's edge, bringing to the fore her feelings of inadequacy since the accident. Before, she had always just taken it for granted that she was a desirable woman. The potency of his masculinity was like having salt poured in the open wound of her self-doubts.

She gestured at the wing chair opposite her. "Please, sit down, Mr. Stanton." She had planned to pull out all the stops on her warmth and charm. Her voice came out as cold as an Arctic wind.

He glanced at the chair, and then at his dusty clothing. "No, thank you, Miss Copperthorne."

Though there was nothing unreasonable about his refusal to take a chair, she felt slighted, and vaguely out of control. In her mind, she had rehearsed her speech with Dace Stanton sitting in that chair, perhaps leaning toward her slightly...but not towering over her, looking restless and impatient and faintly angry. She had not prepared herself for the discomfort his intent gaze made her feel, and she certainly had not prepared herself for the drugging, disorientating effect his scent was having on her. She flinched from the possibility that her father might have been right.

"Sit down," she snapped.

Something flared in his eyes, and she hastily tacked on a "please" in a voice that came out small and desperate.

He hesitated, studying her, obviously as surprised by that small voice as she was humiliated by it. There was a suggestion of a sigh in the deep heave of his chest, and then he moved by her and sat in the chair opposite her.

"Now," she said, attempting pleasantness, "can I get you a cup of tea or something?"

He didn't answer for a moment, and she had the awful feeling he was immensely enjoying some private joke.

"No, thank you," he finally said, and then raised a faintly mocking eyebrow at her. "Assuming I *really* have a choice?"

"Of course you really have a choice," she said, nearly choking on her sweet tone, but determined not to let his sarcasm about being ordered to sit down get her off on the wrong track again. "I suppose you're wondering why you're here?"

Again, that dark, wickedly shaped eyebrow edged upward. "Not to drink tea?" he guessed dryly.

He was not making this easy. Her smile now felt a little tight. "I have a business proposition to discuss with you," she said cautiously. She was rewarded when surprise momentarily overrode his look of studied indifference, but that expression was quickly overtaken by one of suspicion.

"I need someone to ride my horse," she rushed on.

He didn't respond. He seemed to be waiting. Then a surprised light went on in his eyes. "You don't mean me, do you?"

Her nerves were very taut. "Oh, for heaven's sake, Mr. Stanton, you've already guessed that you aren't here to drink tea. Of course I mean you."

"Well, pardon me if I seem a little surprised," he said, and there was a faint edge of impatience in his voice. "Yesterday I got the definite impression you would have had me drawn and quartered, if the lady of the manor were still allowed such luxuries in dealing with the help..."

"Really," she gasped. "There is no need to overstate the facts."

He continued as if she hadn't interrupted, "...for the crime of being reckless with the horseflesh, and today you're asking me to ride an animal who is probably worth more money than I make in several years. Yes, Miss Copperthorne, I'm a little surprised at the change of heart.''

"How do you know how much money my horse is worth?'' she asked absurdly.

"I've seen him around. He's a magnificent animal.'' The last was offered grudgingly.

That grudging statement made her heart rise in her throat. There was a small hope in this seemingly hopeless situation. She knew, beyond a shadow of a doubt, that Dace Stanton had been watching Storm, with the passion a horse like Storm invariably inspired in a lover of horseflesh.

"It's not exactly that I've had a change of heart,'' Cade said carefully.

"Oh,'' he said dryly. "You want me to ride your horse so that you can watch me being reckless, and then you really can have me drawn and——''

"Mr. Stanton, you are being very difficult!''

"Really?'' he said with silky innocence.

"What I was trying to say was that maybe I misjudged the situation yesterday in the first place.''

"Maybe?''

"I didn't have all the facts and I reached the wrong conclusions.'' Humility came very hard to Cadence Copperthorne. "You conducted yourself fairly impressively given the limitations of your mount and your equipment.''

"I think that was a compliment,'' he said wryly. "Thank you.''

"It was a compliment,'' she said seriously. "Many people with years of training don't jump horses that well, and never will. It's a gift—like being able to draw or write. Some people have a natural talent.''

"The kid you have riding him now is not one of them," Dace said. "I don't like the way he rides that horse. He seems scared to death of him."

She nodded wholeheartedly. Unexpectedly, she and Dace Stanton had found common ground. She hated seeing Storm ridden nervously.

"Storm can be unpredictable. He'll go fine for weeks at a time. He'll be obedient and eager and responsive. And then, for a reason I can't determine, he goes wild. He's nearly impossible to control. The changes in mood can happen with incredible swiftness. And then they can be gone just as quickly as they came or last a few days."

Dace smiled a crooked smile that revealed even teeth, brilliantly white against the weathered bronze of his skin. "Sounds as if he's got a bit of personality."

She felt oddly threatened by what that smile did to his face. It washed away the faint cynicism that was stamped into the lines around his mouth, erased the barrier of remoteness that had been in his eyes. It warmed them, and made them sparkle with a devilish charm.

"That 'personality' is why I need to put a very strong rider on him. And that's the proposition. Do you want to ride my horse?"

"Sure."

Her mouth almost dropped open in surprise. "You do?" she asked.

"Actually, I'm glad of the opportunity. It kind of riled me, seeing that kid riding him. Fear doesn't do much for a fine horse." His eyes rested on her face. "Now, I'll bet you weren't ever scared of him, were you?"

She felt the compliment of it, and felt her cheeks grow warm under his steady gaze. "No, I wasn't ever afraid of Storm, Mr. Stanton." If her tone was standoffish, it was because there were those who had thought she should be—her father and Lionel. And maybe they had been right.

"Actually, we don't even have to make it a business arrangement," Dace continued. "I'd be happy to take him out on my own time. I could manage an hour in the mornings, before I start work. Will that suit you until you're back in the saddle yourself?"

The enormity of his misunderstanding hit her. He thought she was asking him for a favor—asking him only to exercise the horse for a little while each day—until she could ride again.

"I won't be riding again," she said stiffly. "The damage to my hip precludes sitting astride a horse."

His face softened, giving her a totally unwanted insight into what he might look like in moments of tenderness, with someone whom he loved, when his guard was down.

"I'm sorry," he said with soft gruffness. "I wasn't aware your injury was permanent."

"Really? I thought everyone on the whole place had nearly talked my accident to death by now." Her tone was shrewish, a deliberate effort to put the ice back in eyes made altogether too devastating by the unexpected understanding in them.

She succeeded in spades. Dace eyed her coolly. "I hate to have to be the one to tell you most of us have better things to do with our time than gossip about you. Naturally, we heard about the accident. And felt bad about it, too. I seem to remember we took up a collection to send you flowers in the hospital."

He looked away from her, and ran a hand through his dark curls. She had the unflattering feeling he might be petitioning heaven to give him patience. When he turned back to her his expression had only the faintest traces of exasperation lingering around the edges.

"Look, my offer stands. I'll ride your horse for you. On my own time. For as long as you need me to."

She didn't even feel particularly flattered that he was prepared to do it on his own time. She didn't need favors or pity from anyone, and least of all from this arrogant, entirely-too-sure-of-himself cowboy!

"You misunderstood me, Mr. Stanton. I wasn't asking you to do anything out of sympathy for me." Her voice was brittle.

That exceedingly brief moment of compatibility that they had shared was gone without a trace, and there didn't seem much hope of its returning.

Dace's posture was no longer relaxed, and his eyes were cold again. "You misunderstood *me*, Miss Copperthorne," he bit out softly, "because I never offered to do anything out of sympathy. I happen to like the look of the animal, and I wouldn't mind giving him a try."

"I'm not looking for somebody to exercise the horse for an hour a day," she stated. It was only a misunderstanding, but there was a strange, electrical tension between them that quickly gave misunderstandings the tone of arguments.

She took a deep breath and managed a very civil tone. "I'm looking for somebody to ride him. Full time. To jump him again, when that time comes."

He stared at her with open astonishment. "Me?"

"Look, there's no need to act as if I've asked you to pilot the next space shuttle." He was looking at her as though she were crazy, and probably because she suspected as much herself she resented it. "I've asked you if you'd like to ride a horse. From what I've seen you already know how to do that, and you're damned good at it, too."

She decided to ignore the stubborn thrust of that square jaw, and concentrate on the fact that he hadn't actually said no. She pushed on. "I think you have an incredible natural talent. I think with training and the right horse——"

He suddenly seemed to realize he hadn't said no. He cut her off abruptly. "I'm a cowboy."

"I know you are. I'm talking about what you could be."

He gave her a hard smile. "I like what I am right now."

She tried to backtrack around his offended pride. "I didn't mean to suggest that being a cowboy didn't have dignity, because I think it does. I mean I think you do. I mean . . . oh, dammit, I mean you could be great!"

"I doubt if you and I define 'great' in quite the same way," he said with slow dignity.

She was now so frustrated she couldn't have been polite and restrained if her very life depended on it. "Where's your ambition, man? Don't you want more out of life than being a hired hand on somebody else's ranch?"

"My ambition, or lack of it, is none of your business," he snapped coldly.

"Okay. Let's try on something that is my business. I'll pay you double whatever you're making now." She knew it was completely the wrong tack to take. Completely. But she didn't know what to do with his brick wall of stubbornness, except try to smash it down.

He eyed her silently.

"Plus give you an apartment over the stables to live in," she tacked on desperately.

"I'm not for sale," he said tersely. "I'm not interested in your money. I am not interested in your apartment. I am not interested in your fancy-pants riding. And I most definitely am not interested in working for you."

"I could fire you," she threatened.

"Yes, ma'am, you could," he agreed without emotion, and then, without waiting for her to say one more word, he unfolded himself from the chair, pivoted on his heel and went out of the door.

". . . if she'd had her cane," Dace told Sloan, "I'm pretty sure she would have thrown it at me."

Sloan's eyes widened, it seemed to Dace more with appreciation than surprise. "Well, I guess you're darned lucky you got out of there without any bruises, boy."

Dace studied that weathered old face for the sarcasm, but it was hard to tell if it was there or not. "I just thought I'd better tell you, because she's going to be on the horn in a few minutes telling you to fire me. And then you can tell her she's too late. That I already quit."

"Now, Dace, don't go being such a hothead. Think things through, son."

"Look, Sloan, I'd rather not quit. I like this job and I like this outfit, but——"

Sloan sighed. "That's not what you need to think through, Dace. You need to think about taking her up on it, for heaven's sake."

"What?" Dace eyed Sloan warily. Hadn't Sloan heard a word he'd said?

"Did you even think about it?" Sloan asked patiently. "Did you even consider it, and what it might mean, or did your foolish pride just jump in there before you even thought about what she offered?"

"I'm no fancy-pants rider, Sloan."

"What are you always jumping my ponies for, then?"

Dace felt himself color. "I don't know. It seems to be in me, in my blood——" He became aware of the admission he was making, stopped himself, stared at his boot. "Aw, hell, Sloan, an old dog can't learn new tricks."

"*I'm* an old dog. You ain't. You're a foolish young pup who just turned down a chance to get paid to learn proper how to do something that you like to do, anyway."

"I don't feel so young, Sloan," he said quietly.

"Look, Dace, I know life handed you a hard deck. You ain't even thirty, and you've buried a wife and a child. Tried bloody hard to bury yourself, too. Well, now I guess you've decided to rejoin the land of the living, except you ain't living. You're coasting. Making the motions. You don't have any friends. You don't see any women. You don't even have a dog. Man, you got to learn to care again.''

''Well, that's sure as hell something she wouldn't be able to teach me.''

''You don't learn to care by taking, Dace, you learn by giving. And you've got something to give her right now. She needs you. You can help her hope again.''

''I don't owe her anything,'' Dace said stubbornly.

''Nope. But you owe me, son.''

Dace felt stunned—and trapped. ''Sloan, don't do this to me.'' It was true. He owed Sloan his very life. But he'd never expected Sloan to call in the debt. He'd thought he'd pay him back in his own time and his own way. ''I can't work for that red-headed witch,'' Dace said, a little desperately.

''Dace, go home and think with your head instead of your mouth.''

From anybody else, that probably would have been an invitation to one heck of a fight. But what could you do about Sloan? The man was over sixty. He had been his own father's best friend. And he'd been the one to pull Dace out of the mire of guilt and grief and booze that he'd fallen into after Janey and Jasmine had died in the fire. Sloan had given him back his life, and now he was requesting one small favor in return.

Small. Ha. It would be no small thing to work with that woman—or that horse.

But at least the horse appealed to him.

CHAPTER THREE

THAT damned cowboy had said no to her.

It was Cade's first thought when she woke up the next morning. It had been stupid to ask Dace, anyway. Her father had been right. It had been a ridiculous idea. Farfetched.

It would probably be impossible to teach someone that stubborn and narrow-minded anything new, anyway.

Still, she disliked losing face—losing, period—born competitor that she was. Well, she would not lose! She was not giving Dace Stanton the least bit of power in her life. She had decided when she was twelve years old she would have an Olympic gold medal one day and she would have it! She could no longer get it herself, and Dace Stanton wasn't going to help her, but there were plenty of fish in the sea.

Imagine thinking, however briefly, that he was the man to do it. She had been blinded by the circumstances. It had been the setting, rather than his actual ability, that had turned her head, made her match him with her horse. It had been the magnificence of an early summer day, and the sea of green grass, and the romance of the cowboy clothes and the flat-out horse that had made her react so dramatically to him, that had made her pair him instinctively with Storm. In an ordinary riding ring doing the very same thing Dace Stanton would have probably looked like an utter idiot.

She heard Storm nicker. The sound was clear in the crisp morning air. It was an unusually friendly sound. Her eyes suddenly opened wide. Storm was in the stable. He never sounded happy when he was confined.

She tossed back the priceless Chinese silk quilt and struggled out of bed. She used the edges of her night table to move around to the window. She shivered. The window was open a crack, and the breeze that stirred the soft white lace of her curtains was chill. It also had that wonderful crisp morning scent. She ignored the chill and flung the window wide open, leaning out, and sucking the morning-scented air into her lungs. The last of her irritation that things hadn't turned out according to her plan was chased away by the full glory of the morning.

The world outside was hazy—the colors muted by the morning mist that floated a few feet off the ground. The sun was just beginning to peep over the hills to the east.

The whole scene was wrapped in an unearthly stillness. The stables, the mist, the far-off hills could have been a painting, except for a sudden flash of movement. Storm. Racing, his tail and head high, to the far reaches of the side paddock, flicking his heels, joyously, and racing back again, celebrating his freedom. He looked like a young colt. The horse was fourteen years old.

She watched, mesmerized by his beauty, his greatness, his magnificence of spirit. And then, startled, she wondered how he'd got out. Last night, she had made a mournful tour of the stables, and he had been in, irritable and restive.

For a moment she felt afraid. He might have kicked his way through the door. Or managed somehow to jump over the lower gate of his box stall. He might be hurt...

He neighed again, and she smiled ruefully. It was not the sound of an injured horse. In fact, Storm was acting very much as if he was showing off, which he enjoyed doing immensely, when he wasn't in one of his baffling, uncontrollable moods.

She caught a movement in the shadow of the stable, and focused on it. The figure was unmistakable. Dace Stanton was leaning casually in the doorframe of the open box stall, his thumbs hooked in his pockets.

He had let out her horse! The man was really insufferable. Hastily she turned from the window and to her wardrobe. Carelessly, she pulled a gray hooded sweatshirt over the sheerness of her shortie summer pyjamas. She crammed her uncooperative limbs impatiently into a pair of faded jeans, gave the wild tangle of her hair a shake and a finger-comb, then grabbed her cane and crashed out of her room.

He was still there when she rounded the corner, still standing with one big shoulder braced against the doorframe, his back to her.

"What are you doing here?" she snapped. She was irritated because she had come. The man did have an undeniable chemistry. In the safe haven of her room she could picture him as an utter idiot. In the light of reality the man couldn't have looked like an idiot if he rode a horse backward with a dunce's cap on his head.

He turned and glanced over his shoulder at her. His eyes were shadowed by the brim of his hat, which he touched briefly with his fingers.

"Morning, ma'am." For a moment longer than could have been considered proper his eyes rested on the tiny silk bow and the lacy neck of her pyjamas that showed under the V of her sweatshirt. Then he turned and looked back at the antics of the horse.

"Did you let this horse out of his stall?" she demanded.

"Yes, ma'am, I did. He didn't seem very happy inside."

"I don't see that that is any concern of yours," she said waspishly. "Are you in charge of unhappy animals? If you went to a zoo would you be letting all the tigers out?"

"Probably," Dace said, his unperturbed tone perturbing her unbearably.

"We keep Storm inside at night because we are trying to get him accustomed to confined spaces. At shows he has to be stabled in a confined area."

"Exactly how long have you been trying that?" Dace asked, unimpressed. His eyes drifted to her face.

She bit her lip. Long enough to know it wasn't working. "I asked you what you were doing here," she reminded him.

"I wanted to have a closer look at the horse."

Her heart jumped and she scanned that impassive face for some clue of what had brought him out here at dawn's first light. His face told her nothing, though for some reason she could have looked at it for a long, long time. Instead, she made herself appear to fasten her attention to Storm. She

noticed there was a morning-fresh scent clinging to
Dace that was nearly as perturbing as her inability
to get a rise out of him.

Storm, in one of those moments of affection that
had won her devotion to him, despite the other
problems with his personality, suddenly stopped
dead in his tracks, and lifted his nose. Then, having
caught her scent, he wheeled back to the stable,
came at them at a dead run, screeched to a halt in
front of them, and dropped his large head against
her bosom.

She scratched his ears obediently, and a sigh of
contentment escaped her. After a moment, she
looked up to see Dace Stanton studying her, something in his eyes that she had not seen before.
Puzzlement? And a kind of empathy...

She was sorry she had let her guard down, sorry
that a tenderness had slipped out of her, and that
he had seen it. If she was soft, people took it as an
invitation to pity her. If she was abrasive and hard
they kept their distance and she kept some remnant
of her dignity. She shoved Storm away from her,
and glared challengingly at Dace. His expression
was bland.

"I don't suppose you've changed your mind,
have you?" she asked crisply. If he thought she was
going to beg him to ride her horse, he had another
think coming. Arrogant cowboy. Acting as if he
owned the place. Still, seeing Dace and Storm
together in such close proximity did reawaken that
same overwhelmingly strong sense of rightness that
she had been struck by when she had seen Dace
jump for the first time.

"He's a beautiful animal," Dace commented, not
answering her question at all.

"On his good days, he's very, very good." She sighed. "But on his bad days he's horrid."

Dace laughed at her paraphrasing of the old nursery rhyme. She was caught unprepared for the sound of his laughter. It melted into the magic of the morning, rolling like the mist, putting the brightness of the rising sun to shame.

She looked at him. She hadn't realized there was an ever-present hurt lurking in the cool pools of his eyes, until the laughter washed it away. Wounded, she guessed, and was somehow unsurprised. For a reason she didn't know, some unspeakable wound seemed to be an element in greatness of spirit. She suspected that Storm, too, was irrevocably scarred by some past event.

Her eyes flicked from the horse to the man, and back again. Again, she could feel it, the sizzle of their energy, the potential of them as a team. She wanted it so badly that she wanted to scream, to shake him, to make him see. Some of the discipline of her long years of working with skittish horses came to her aid now. No fast movements. Quiet. Calm. No rushing fences.

Besides, it did not do to want things too badly. She had no intention of giving Dace Stanton that kind of power over her.

"I thought I might have a look at the room that goes with the job you offered me."

"Certainly," she said, trying desperately to keep a rein on her eagerness. One false move, and she suspected he'd bolt. She stole a look at his face as they passed through the doors into the dimness of the stable. He didn't want to be here. But he was. She did not dare even ask him why.

"The suite is through that door, at the top of those stairs. Nobody's using it. It was for my head groom."

"What happened to the groom?" Dace had moved very close to her, his eyes scanning her face.

She could see, reflected in his eyes, that her hurt was obvious to him, and it embarrassed her. She schooled her face into careful uncaring. "He was made a better offer."

She didn't add that the offer had been made by her ex-fiancé.

Dace nodded slowly but his eyes didn't leave her face, seeing things she did not want him to see. Then he turned from her abruptly, and opened the door, standing back for her to precede him.

A feeling of humiliation washed through her. She wished she could just drop through the floor. She wished she were back in her bed, her covers pulled over her head.

"Stairs are very difficult for me," she choked out, her eyes glued on a piece of straw on the floor. Not impossible, but difficult. Besides, she hated the way she looked trying to mount stairs. Her father had installed a lift chair for her in the house.

Because she wasn't looking at him, she didn't even see him coming.

Suddenly, he was just there in front of her. One strong arm closed like a steel band around her shoulders, and the other slid under her knees. The cane clattered from her hands and in a split second she was being cradled against the hard wall of his chest, and she looked into his eyes, only to find an expression in them that seemed as astounded as her own.

"Put me down," she demanded. "I've seen the room. I——"

He ignored her, went up the stairs. The exertion did not change his breathing, though to her intense embarrassment her breaths were coming in quick, indignant little gasps.

"Put me down this instant or I'll——"

"You can't fire me. I don't even work for you yet."

That "yet" stole her protests momentarily. She'd lost a weapon. He'd guessed that no matter how angry he made her she wouldn't pull rank on Sloan. So that "yet" might indicate he was considering working for her, directly.

Unfortunately as soon as she stopped protesting she became aware of the implacable hardness of his chest, and aware of the rock-hard rippling of the muscled arm beneath her thighs.

She banged his chest angrily with the flat of her hand.

He went to the top of the stairs, strode across the sun-splashed room and dumped her unceremoniously on the couch. He took in the red stain of her cheeks with amusement.

Her fists curled into balls of impotent rage at her sides. "I hate being touched," she stormed.

He looked totally unintimidated. "Every man's nightmare," he commented dryly. "A beautiful woman who hates to be touched."

"I didn't mean it like that," she gasped, flustered.

"Oh. So you do like to be touched." His eyebrows had arched wickedly upward.

"Don't you mock me. You know exactly what I mean."

"I don't have a clue what you're talking about," he denied flatly.

"You would never treat a woman who didn't limp with such audacious familiarity. I will not be treated like an invalid," she clarified, her voice an angry hiss.

To her chagrin, he laughed. He actually threw back his head, and laughed into the face of her rage.

He finally managed to stop laughing, and looked at her solemnly. Then suddenly he stooped and took her chin, forcing her to meet the steady, stripping gaze of his eyes.

"As a matter of fact, Miss Copperthorne, I have been known to be audaciously familiar with members of the female persuasion. My past is dotted with incidents of audacious familiarity. In fact, I think I was only in grade three the first time I stole a kiss from a girl I didn't even know..."

"Oh, stop it," she demanded, trying to squirm away from his hold. He held fast to her chin, forcing her to look into those eyes that danced with a light of pure devilment. For a moment she was dreadfully afraid he was planning to demonstrate his stolen kiss technique. She was willing to bet it had improved since the third grade. What a repulsive thought. The man was a caveman. Why on earth was her heart hammering like that?

Then the light of debauchery died in his eyes. "As for treating you like an invalid, I forgot entirely you were an 'invalid,' which by the way is your choice of phrase, not mine. That's why I opened the door for you, and expected you to go up first. Nobody who is with you for any length of time is going to give much thought to your leg or your limp. I find it keeps me pretty busy just watching out for your tongue.''

Her mouth fell open in shock. She glared at him. She slapped his hand away from her chin, folded her arms across her chest and looked coldly over his shoulder.

"Given the circumstances, I think I've been more than civil to you this morning."

He straightened and looked around the room with interest. And then his eyes came back to rest on her. "Do you think you managed to be civil for ten or twenty seconds because it's your nature, or because you want something?" he asked softly.

She snapped him a coldly killing look before looking away again. She shoved her nose toward the ceiling. "It's my nature."

She wanted to murder him when he laughed again. It was on the tip of her tongue to tell him he was fired, but no, that would be too good for him, and besides, he'd already pointed out that he didn't work for her "yet." She decided she wanted to tie him down on an anthill and cover him with honey. Oh, she detested the fact that he was absolutely right. She should really try to be nice. She needed him. And hated needing him.

He turned his broad back on her and went to explore the small apartment.

She watched him narrowly as he strode from room to room. She willed herself to feel only professional calm, to view him with detachment. The man who might give her back her dream, ride her horse... but it wasn't working. When he'd touched her, carried her in those magnificently strong arms, the physical side of her had surged to life, tingling with an electrical awareness of his masculinity. In-

tellectually, she did her utmost to cut that off, and
yet she could not prevent herself from appreciating
the clean lines of his leg muscles in his molded
jeans, the broad sweep of his shoulders, the incredible midnight blue of his eyes. And something
even stronger, and certainly more distressing, than
anger twinged deep within her.

What was it? Yearning? Desire? The ache of re-
pressed loneliness? Whatever it was, it was
dangerous.

She forced herself to think of Lionel, to remember his treachery in agonizing detail. She held
two vivid pictures of him in her mind; one of his
flushed and joyous face, when he'd pulled her from
Storm after the best ride they'd ever had. In that
delirious moment, swept away by the emotion of
the victory, he'd asked her to marry him.

It had seemed natural enough at the time. They
had spent nearly every waking moment in each
other's company. They had shared the same obsession; the same goals; the same interests. Everything they had done revolved around horses,
competitions, the far-off goal of places on the
Olympic team. It didn't take the pain away to know,
now, that what they had felt was not so much a
passion for each other as a residue of passion from
the sport, and its inherent exhilaration.

Her other picture of Lionel had been snapped
with her mind two short weeks later. He had visited
her in the hospital, but his eyes had had a look in
them she could not bear. It wasn't just sympathy,
it was revulsion. He was an athlete, incapable of
transcending his world of strength and movement
to find out if they had shared anything else.

She would never forget Lionel letting a look of unguarded horror slide over the perfection of his good looks, when she had explained what they would do to her hip, when she'd told him bluntly she would always use a cane, when she'd told him, her voice faltering, that she would never ride a horse again. She had not even been able to tell him the rest.

He had come a few more times, dutifully. She hated him for that—for making her feel as if she was just a pair of legs, and without them her life was over, she was worthless.

Dace Stanton came out of the back reaches of the apartment, and she eyed him, satisfied that she had the maturity to deal swiftly with such a juvenile thing as a physical attraction before it developed into anything that could hurt her again. Besides, he'd probably dismissed her handicap with such ease precisely because he didn't think of her as the kind of woman who would interest him physically.

"We could talk," he conceded.

Lionel and his betrayal were still fresh in her brain. "Yes," she said, "we could talk." That much did not require trust.

He moved toward her as though he might actually try to pick her up again. She quelled him with a look.

"I'll wait for you outside," he stated.

"Naturally, I'll want you to sign a contract." They were sitting on the flagstoned breakfast terrace overlooking the pool.

Dace managed to make the area look like a set from a movie—he was too large, and too *real* somehow for white cane furniture and plump yellow pillows. She was forced to notice, again, that he was a man unintimidated by his surroundings. He seemed infinitely at home with the opulence of cut-glass flower vases on rattan tables, with the feel of fine Wedgwood in his big, work-roughened hands.

She was oddly taken with the look of that strong, weathered hand against fine porcelain. There was a fineness in his movement, in the ease with which he handled the delicate bone china, that defied his large size. If his hands were this good on the reins, this light, this sensitive . . .

A renegade thought blasted through her brain, of how those hands might feel against the porcelain of a woman's skin, how they might guide the reins of her passion . . .

"I'm not signing a contract," he said. His voice was smooth and sure. As if this was not even open to negotiation.

She pulled her gaze from his hands, and met his eyes. They were watchful, but unworried, on her face.

"I need a contract," she insisted. "I'll be investing a great deal of time and money in you. I think I should be able to protect myself against your just up and walking away."

His eyes never left her face. "Miss Copperthorne," he said softly and solemnly, "when a man feels like up and walking away, you're best to just let him. You see, you can't own a man's soul. His spirit. He can only give you that freely. And, if he isn't giving that part of himself to you, there's no point having him. Do you understand what I'm saying?"

Unfortunately, she did. She realized she still wanted guarantees from life. She should know better by how.

Still, she studied him with a trace of skepticism. "Why are you doing this? Frankly, you seem more interested in the apartment than the work that we'll be doing."

He was here, and he'd said he'd do it, but she didn't feel as if he was offering her his heart and soul.

"For the pleasure of your company?" he parried.

She flushed. Why was *she* doing this? Exposing herself to the ruthless digs of this overpowering cowboy?

"Does it matter why?" he asked softly. "Maybe for the money. Maybe for the change. Maybe for the challenge. Maybe it is for the apartment."

She felt doubtful and must have looked it.

"Miss Copperthorne, this was your great idea in the first place. I like the horse, and I'm willing to give this an honest try. I'll give you my word on that, and my handshake. In that world," he nodded off past the hedges toward the dust rising from the corrals, "that's the best kind of contract to have. I can usually tell just about everything I need to know from the way a person shakes hands."

He rose, turning the tables on her, concluding *her* interview.

He looked down at her, his eyes unreadable, a trace of a solemn smile toying at the edges of his wind-roughened lips. Slowly, he extended his hand.

For a moment, she only stared at it, afraid to take it. Afraid he might know something of her that she didn't want him to know.

Oh, for heaven's sake, she chided herself. She wasn't buying any silly cowboy corn pone. She struggled to her feet, in defiance of the deep blue eyes that told her it was all right to remain seated.

She extended her own hand to him, and he took it. Her hand disappeared, small and white, into the fold of his, large and brown. She felt a shocked sense of her own femininity. He shook her hand firmly. And it was true. Everything that he was, was in that handshake. It conveyed unwavering strength and compelling energy. In that handshake was a promise of something solid and reliable. And then instead of releasing her hand he held it for a moment, letting her feel the texture of his skin, the callused history written on his palms. Letting her feel the energy grow, until it tingled up her arm. This too was a message of a man who was as innately sensuous as he was strong.

She pulled her hand abruptly away from him, feeling singed, feeling the heat of that singe burning in her cheeks.

Without taking his eyes from her, he settled his cowboy hat over his dark hair, and tugged the brim low over his brow. She could not tell from his unwavering gaze if he felt the same sizzling intensity as she did.

"Well, Miss Copperthorne?"

She gasped. "Well, what?" she stammered.

A lazy, amused smile tugged at his lips. She was glad he didn't smile more. It made him even more dangerous, made him appear wickedly and carelessly sexy.

"Do we have a deal?"

Something in her warned her about making deals with devils, but in a flash the look in his eyes was gone. They became hooded, faintly remote. He was just a man. They were just talking about a job.

"Yes, we have a deal," she said, her voice not nearly so strong or snappy as she would have liked. "Would Monday be all right? To start?"

He nodded.

"You can move your things into the stable any time."

He shrugged. "That won't be much of a job." He turned away, and then turned back. "Thanks for the coffee, Miss Copperthorne."

"Cade," she astounded herself by saying.

His eyes narrowed. "Cade," he repeated, rolling it off his lips thoughtfully. He nodded and turned and strode away, moving by the pool, cutting through the hedge.

In his stride and in the way he had said her name, she knew two things. He was not *just* a man. It was not *just* a job. Something bigger was happening, was bound to happen. There was passion here. Passion in the way she felt about jumping, and in the way he felt about horses. It was hard to work around something like that and not be affected by it. Look at her and Lionel. Of course, when it came right down to it, it was a mistake to try and transfer that passion to something else. Of course, when it came right down to it, though, passion was a hard one to tame, to keep in its proper compartments.

Suddenly she realized she was feeling something she hadn't felt for a long time: that edgy nervous feeling in the pit of her stomach that she felt before a big show. A combination of raw nerves and excitement, of fear and challenge. She looked at the place where Dace had disappeared through the hedge, and she smiled. It was scary as hell, but dammit, it still felt good to be alive.

"I guess maybe I'll give it a shot with Miss Copperthorne's horse," Dace told Sloan casually, taking his saddle off the tack-room wall, slipping his fingers under the horn, and swinging it over his shoulder.

Sloan shrugged, wisely deciding not to make too much of it, but Dace didn't miss the satisfied look that gleamed briefly in his eye.

Dace sat for a long time out on the leaning porch of his small cabin. His land was three miles from Copperthorne's. The cabin was awful—hot, small, musty. No running water, or electricity. He'd lived here since the fire. Four years. The apartment over the stables would seem like a penthouse in comparison to how he was living now.

He supposed Sloan was right. It was time to re-enter the land of the living.

He smoked one cigar, and then another, watching the setting sun, feeling its gold on his face.

He wondered why she called herself Cade when he personally thought Cadence was a far more suiting name. Feminine, strong. He sighed. He felt restless. He picked up a stick he'd been twirling, and brushed absently at the dust at his feet. A name formed.

He scowled down at it, and then, for a reason he didn't quite know, wrote his own name beneath it. He studied the two names for a long time, and then a light went on in his head.

"I'll be damned," he said with disbelief. He tossed the stick into the night, looked incredulously once more at the names, and then impatiently erased them with a swipe of his foot.

CHAPTER FOUR

ON FRIDAY, Cade had watched, surreptitiously, as Dace moved a few things from the back of a dilapidated pickup truck into the apartment above the stable.

By Saturday, she knew the awful truth. She could not wait until Monday. If she did, they would have to spend Monday outfitting him, and couldn't actually start work until Tuesday. But if they outfitted him today...

She knew she was being ridiculous. Several times, she told herself just how ridiculous she was being, and forced herself to sit down with a book. Then she would gaze unseeingly at the pages for several minutes, and then her eyes would drift to the bedroom window, and then the next thing she knew she had levered herself up, and was back at that window, peeping out from behind the curtains, trying to discern if she could see him moving around above the stable. Ridiculous. But there was a knot of anxiety in her stomach. As if, if she waited until Monday, something might go wrong. He might change his mind. He might move back out of the stable as quickly as he'd moved in.

Finally, she could bear it no longer. She'd just go over there, and check out his mood, lay her anxieties to rest. Her mind made up, she snatched a potted plant off the night table beside her bed. What could be more natural than for her to bring him a little housewarming gift?

She'd actually forgotten all about those narrow steep stairs that led up to his place, but having come this far she found herself unable to turn back, and unable to humiliate herself by yelling up the stairs that she was here.

She nestled the potted plant safely in the crook of her arm, hooked her cane over her opposite forearm, grabbed the railing, took a deep breath and went up. She arrived at the top breathless, flushed and sweating. She had made more noise than a steam locomotive, but thankfully he had not opened the door to investigate.

Neither did he open the door when she knocked on it. Not to be thwarted at this point, she gave his door a couple of good hits with her cane.

And for some reason almost tumbled over backward with surprise when the door was flung open and he stood there, wearing only blue jeans, his chest naked and damp, his hair beaded with water.

He had a towel in his hand and he casually began roughing his hair with it. He looked at her inquiringly, not in the least self-conscious about his big, beautiful body—in fact, she suspected, rather enjoying her discomfort.

"I brought you this." She thrust the plant at him, and he reached for it with his free hand. Then both of them stood staring at the plant.

It registered with her that she'd brought him an African violet and that he looked absurd holding the dainty, dusty-looking purple plant against his naked chest. He didn't seem to know what to do with the plant...or her. His gaze moved from the plant to her face just as she was trying to blot some of the sweat from her forehead with the back of her sleeve. She dropped her arm abruptly, but he looked beyond her to the stairs, and comprehension of how much effort she had made to get here dawned, somewhat baffled, in his eyes.

"Could you hang on a second?" He motioned her to the couch. "I'll be right back." He looked at the plant once more, then set it down on his kitchen counter.

Somewhere she heard a running tap being shut off. She looked around his apartment with the cautious interest of a Peeping Tom who was trying to glean some details about him. She was disappointed. The place was cheerful, sun streaming in the front and gable windows and reflecting off the hardwood floors. There were a few scatter-rugs, a nondescript calico sofa, a television, VCR, and stereo. All, if she recalled correctly, came with the place—the homyness had a decorator's hand in it. Dace had not added anything of his own. Not even a photograph. There was a bedroom off the living room and she craned her neck to see in. She wondered if there was a picture beside his bed . . .

"Thanks for the plant. My grandmother used to have one like it."

She jumped guiltily, then turned to look at him. His tone hinted that he found her friendly gesture slightly surprising and slightly suspect. But his face was impassive as he pulled a crisp cotton shirt over the bronzed perfection of his shoulders. He buttoned it, the hard deep plane of his chest, then the hard hollow of his stomach, disappearing from her view. He unselfconsciously tucked his shirttails into his jeans, and she realized she had been staring. Her eyes moved up to his face and he was watching her with amusement, one side of his mouth quirked upward.

"You're welcome," she said stiltedly.

"I'd offer you something, but I haven't laid in any supplies yet. I was just on my way into town."

"Were you?" She couldn't believe her good fortune, even though she had to screw up her nerve to take advantage of it. "Do you think we could go together? I need to pick up a number of things at the equestrian shop."

He hesitated, and she read faint suspicion into his steady gaze.

She deliberately dropped her eyes. "I can't carry heavier items by myself."

It was the first time she'd used pity to her advantage, and she was rather pleased with the results. She sneaked a look at him, and saw he looked abashed by both his suspicion and his hesitation. Good. If he was ashamed of himself and feeling sorry for her, he wouldn't even think that the staff would offer to carry her purchases out for her, which of course they always did.

"While we're here," she said a little over an hour later, "we might as well pick up some things for you."

They were in a very posh riding shop called English Leather, and Dace had spared the briefest of glances to the riding attire, and now was looking at saddles. And the price tags on saddles. He lifted one that she knew to be particularly expensive and almost physically winced at its lightness.

He turned to her. "What?"

She gave him her brightest smile. "This is Daniel. He works here. He'll help you pick out some riding clothes."

Daniel stepped forward with a pair of cream-colored breeches. "Sir, these are our best riding pants," he said. "Slim-line, four-way stretch, reinforced——"

"Would you excuse us a minute?" Dace asked grimly. He reached by Daniel and his hand bit into her shoulder. She found herself unceremoniously backed into a corner, blocked from Daniel's wide-eyed gaze by a set of huge shoulders.

"You want to tell me what's going on?" he hissed dangerously.

"Nothing," she said, widening her eyes to rounded innocence. "I just thought since we were here——"

"Would you cut the garbage? This is why we're here, isn't it?"

"Of course not——"

A hand flashed over her shoulder and thumped into the wall behind her, and he leaned his weight against it, making her feel trapped physically, as well as trapped by the angry sparks in his blue eyes.

"You'd better be straight with me, Cade—or I'll walk out that door and never come back. I'm not going to work with you if you're going to be sneaky and manipulative. I knew the minute you brought me that plant you were up to something." His voice was flat and hard.

"I was not! It was just a nice neighborly gesture——"

"Like hell!"

"I am capable of such gestures, you know!"

"If you are, I haven't seen any evidence of it." His voice was a low, threatening rumble. "Come clean, Miss Copperthorne."

She sighed. And even felt a little ashamed of herself, mostly because she knew he was entirely justified in his anger. She had got him in here under false pretenses.

"I'm sorry," she managed. She seemed to be getting more practice than she wanted in being humble these days. She took a deep breath and decided to be entirely honest. "I started getting anxious. And I started to feel really excited about working on Monday. And then I realized we'd have to get you outfitted. And that it wasn't going to be easy to get you into a habit. Dace, I am sor——"

"A what? It's not going to be easy to get me into a *what*?" he asked with soft thunder.

"A habit——"

"A habit," he repeated ominously. "*Nuns* wear habits. Not cowboys. Not this cowboy. Not ever."

She found his ferocity totally intimidating. She wanted to duck under that well-muscled arm and run for cover from the accusation in his eyes. Instead, she lifted her chin a notch, and met his eyes dead-on.

It would, she decided, get things off on entirely the wrong foot if he thought she'd shrink up like a violet every time he used that lethally soft tone of voice on her.

"It's not that kind of habit. You needn't act as if I'm asking you to wear women's lingerie," she informed him stoutly. "A habit is just a kind of uniform for riding. It consists of a jacket and some breeches——"

"Breeches," he muttered. "Sure. And maybe a shirt with a little lace at the wrists. Thank heaven I don't have enough hair to put in a ponytail."

"Oh! You have the wrong idea, entirely!" She noticed it was a whole rack of breeches that had her hemmed in on the left. She snatched a pair off the rack and held them out to him. "See——"

His arm came unglued from the wall and he backed away as though she were proffering a skunk.

"I'm not wearing those," he informed her, eyeing her like a wary animal.

"Surely you had realized you wouldn't be wearing jeans, Dace."

"Women think about what they're going to wear," he informed her caustically. "I hadn't given it a thought." He eyed the jodhpurs with disdain. "And I don't want to think about it now."

"This is an entirely different kind of riding, Dace," she said. She sensed his anger lessening, and she used a soothing tone, the kind she might use on Storm when he was riled. "Jeans would be awfully uncomfortable. They bunch at the knee. They don't stretch over——" She stopped, an outrageous red burning hot up her neck toward her cheeks.

"Look, I guess maybe in the back of my head somewhere I knew I might have to wear something else if I ever go in a show or something, but not on my home ground. I'm not wearing any fancy pants around here."

"Nobody's going to see you, Dace," she crooned, thinking he was concerned about his cowhand friends giving him a hard time.

"You are," he said flatly.

She felt surprise jolt through her. Surely he didn't care what she thought about him? She realized the very idea made her feel warm inside.

"I happen to think there's nothing more masculine than a man in breeches," she reassured him huskily.

He eyed her narrowly, then sighed. "Look, Cade, the truth of it is that the corrals aren't very far from the stables, and you probably can't begin to imagine the kind of comments some of those tough old cowpokes might make if they saw me in . . ." he waved a disdainful hand at the breeches she was holding " . . . those," he finished tersely.

It was the cowhands he was worried about. She was trying very hard to keep a straight face, but she lost the battle. A low chuckle slipped out, and when his face darkened warningly the chuckle dissolved into laughter. The more she tried to check it, the more it bubbled out.

"It's not funny," he told her, but she could see a grin tugging at his own mouth, and she laughed harder.

"Oh, give me those," he said finally, and snatched the riding breeches from her hands, and stood looking at her. Her laughter dried up in her throat, and she wiped hastily at a tear that had washed down her cheek. His eyes were suddenly entirely without humor, intense and stripping on her face. There was something of shocked discovery in those eyes, and then a deep, licking fire of passion.

"You're a beautiful woman when you let go, Cade Copperthorne."

Cadence felt stunned. Her mind tried to tell her she was wrong, but, even as it did, she could feel a fine tension roll along her spine, an anticipation brace her stomach. He was going to kiss her. Standing right here, in the middle of English Leather, with Daniel hovering with undisguised interest behind a nearby boot shelf, Dace Stanton was going to kiss her. She ordered herself to move away from him, but nature had commandeered her body, and instead of moving away she felt herself lean imperceptibly closer, felt her eyes closing and her lips parting——

He leapt back, with much the same wariness that he had used when she'd held out the jodhpurs to him.

She straightened, humiliated, but saw no pity in his eyes, or censure, either. She saw confusion that seemed to match her own . . . and she saw that mysterious light still smoldered there.

She drew herself up haughtily. Well, that had been a near miss! As if she wanted to be kissed by somebody who had been practicing his charms since he'd been in the third grade! He'd probably told his pigtailed conquests back then that they were beautiful, too.

"Er— I'll try these on," he said, not taking his eyes from her face.

"Yes. All right."

He spun abruptly away from her, and almost bumped into Daniel. "Bring me a couple of pairs of these," he ordered crisply, and gave his size. He disappeared into a fitting room. She pushed her luck a little and had Daniel bring him in several pairs of riding boots to try as well.

He emerged, a while later, dressed once more in his crisp jeans and open-necked shirt. The expression on his face was remote. She didn't dare let on that she had hoped he might come out and show the riding clothes to her.

"Wrap anything that fitted," she whispered at Daniel as Dace marched by her.

Dace turned to her as he pressed his shoulder against the door to leave. "I'm going to get my groceries, and then some lunch," he said, quietly. "I'll meet you back at the truck in an hour."

She nodded, unable to be offended that she had not been invited to lunch. By the look on his face she was fortunate to be getting a ride home. The door crashed shut behind him.

A few seconds later it squeaked back open. "If you have them set aside anything you buy, I'll drop by later and carry it out to the truck for you."

She stilled Daniel's protest with one quickly lifted finger. "Thanks, Dace," she said demurely. She was quite pleased with her impassive tone. It was not the voice of a woman who stood in the middle of a public shop and recklessly invited kisses. Still, she tucked Dace's reluctant thoughtfulness into a secret place deep within her and allowed herself to be warmed by it.

Cadence was up at the crack of dawn on Monday morning, but she waited for a decent hour to head across to the stable. At about seven-thirty she finally limped casually across the lawn. She'd told Dace eight, but she was champing at the bit, ready and raring to go.

She went into the tack room and put on coffee. The tack room was large, and she'd always used part of it as a lounge, too. There was a small fridge, and a sink, and an old overstuffed sofa. One entire wall was covered, floor to ceiling, with the rainbow array of her ribbons. Another had been shelved in to hold her trophies.

Once she'd spent most of her life in this dark, comfy room that smelled overbearingly and beautifully of leather. She'd pinned her first ribbon on that wall ten years ago. Lionel had kissed her for the first time on that couch. She'd slept in here when her horses were sick.

A feeling of nostalgia was creeping over her.

"Good morning."

She flinched when Dace poked his head around the door, feeling as if she had been found at her most vulnerable, her most unguarded. It made her slam up her walls twice as high.

"This is where the coffee smell is coming from," he said, coming in. "I make lousy coffee."

He came around the door, and she noticed he wasn't wearing any of his new clothes.

She had hardly let him have a sip of coffee when she said, "Well, are you ready to go to work?"

He set down the coffee cup. "Sure. Your coffee is even lousier than mine."

She recognized that she had an incredible urge to fight with him. To take that innocuous remark and turn it into the Third World War. And then she recognized something else: she was nervous as well as nostalgic, and she didn't want him to guess that, either.

"There's tack over there under the brass plate that says 'Ohmylady.' Could you get it?"

Dace went and pulled the saddle from its tree. He hefted it experimentally on one arm.

"Geez," he muttered. "There can't be enough leather in this overgrown bicycle seat to make a wallet." With a shake of his head he removed the bridle from its peg, and turned to look at her.

She was glowering furiously at him. Overgrown bicycle seat? "This is the sport of kings," she said with tight reserve. Actually, she thought maybe that phrase referred to racing, but she had always felt it *should* refer to show jumping. Anyway, how dared he mock what was most precious to her?

"Lead on, then, King Copperthorne," he suggested dryly. "Or do you prefer Princess?"

"I think I'd prefer to have stayed in bed," she snapped, and stamped outside, thumping her cane down vigorously.

"That's fairly obvious," he drawled from behind her. "Are you always like this in the morning?"

They went out into the sunshine, and she turned with a toss of her head and glared at him. "Like what?"

His eyes strayed to her hair. She felt a few strands of it still hissing angrily about her head, before they floated down to rest on her shoulders. Out of the corner of her eye she could see that the sun was dancing off her hair, making it a far more outrageous red than it really was.

He muttered something under his breath as he moved by her. For an astounded minute, she thought he might have said "beautiful," but from the flinty cast of his profile she realized that wasn't even a remote possibility.

Unless he'd meant the horse, which he was looking at with liking.

"She's a pretty little thing," he said, setting the saddle on the top bar of the fence, and moving over to the roan mare who was tied to it.

He *had* meant the horse.

Still, watching his sure, affectionate way with the mare, Cadence felt the sharpness of her earlier nervousness dulling. She realized she had to get a grip—to try for a more cooperative attitude, or she wouldn't even have an outside chance at her gold medal. And, even though she wouldn't be riding, she now had something of her old beloved world back, and before she had had nothing.

"I'm sorry I was snappish." Here she was apologizing to him *again*.

His astounded expression made her struggle with an impulse to start snapping all over again. Instead, she squared her shoulders and turned to the horse.

"Her name's Ohmylady," she volunteered, joining him, and petting the mare's nose. "I usually end up calling her Ohmy. She's small for an open jumper, but she's got a lot of heart. She's a joy to ride because she's really sweet tempered and she just does what she's asked. Always. No surprises."

"Part quarter horse?"

Cadence nodded. "Yes. A lot of the best open jumpers are bits of this and bits of that. She's quarter and thoroughbred, actually." She noticed, with blessed relief, that they were finally slipping into the narrow neutral area of their shared interest in horses.

She began to groom the mare. "I'll be hiring a groom to do this some time this week."

"I like looking after my horses myself," Dace said with that note of formidable stubbornness she was beginning to recognize. He had picked up a currycomb and was working Ohmylady's other side.

"I do, too," she agreed. "But with five horses that can be tough. Especially on a show schedule.

Sometimes I'd have two or three horses at a show with me, in case one was injured or soured. A groom's pretty much a necessity in that situation.''

By the time they had finished grooming, they were getting along quite companionably, though Cadence wished he'd be a little more cautious with those big shoulders. He'd brushed up against her three times now, and each time the heated shock of it had stolen the words right off her lips. Well, okay, he was attractive. But he wouldn't be interested in her in that way, so she would just file it and avoid his shoulders.

Her confidence grew. She knew what she was talking about, and she liked talking about anything that had to do with her horses and show jumping. And Dace actually seemed to be listening with interest, not a shadow of impatience or boredom clouding the utterly too intense blue of his eyes.

He didn't even look too troubled when she explained to him that they would have to do an incredible amount of flat work before he could progress to jumping.

"I think we're ready to go to work, Mr. Stanton," she told him. She explained the different mount to him, then stepped back, and smiled as he vaulted lithely into the saddle. An athlete.

She spent most of the morning just familiarizing him with the difference in seat and style, and reining. As soon as they had started to work the tension had completely dissipated between them. The focus was now on something else, and Cade had an incredible single-mindedness of focus. As did Dace, she noted. His feel was even better than she could have hoped, and he learned with incredible quickness. They progressed to basic dressage flat work very quickly.

She glanced at her watch a little later and was astounded to see that they had been working for three hours. It was an intoxicating glimmer of old times, old times when she had been so absorbed in what she was doing that hours could disappear as though they were minutes. But, now that she was aware of the passage of time, she was also aware that the persistent ache in her hip had been trying to tell her she was overdoing it for some time.

"Let's call it a morning," she suggested.

He nodded, stopped the horse and she explained the dismount to him. He executed it as though he had never ridden any other way.

"We can call it a day, if you want," she said, "or we could work a little more this afternoon with a different horse."

"I'd like to work this afternoon." He frowned at her. "Are you all right?"

She could feel his eyes fastened with sudden awareness on her face.

"Oh, yes, I'm fine," she claimed proudly.

"You're a fine liar," he said. "You're almost falling over, Cade."

"I am not."

"Are you supposed to stand on your leg for that long?"

"It's my hip that was hurt, not my leg," she evaded.

"Just answer the question."

"It's none of your business!" This was exactly the kind of attention no woman wanted from a devilishly attractive man.

"Look, I'm not going to be responsible for your enthusiasm overcoming your common good sense. I can tell you're in pain, and I doubt that it's doing your hip any good."

"I'll be responsible for that!" she informed him.

"Ha. If there's one thing that life has taught me it's that bad-tempered redheads are not responsible. Especially when they're having a little fit of temper."

"I am not!" she said, aghast.

"Whatever. I've decided I'm not quite up to riding this afternoon, after all."

She was not fooled for a second. Here was a man who'd in all likelihood spent most of his life on a horse. He was probably tougher than saddle leather, and three hours astride would barely warm him up.

It occurred to her, suddenly, she should be thankful to him. Her hip was now thrumming with pain, and she wasn't sure how she would make it to the house, let alone be able to stand again all afternoon. But she was beyond the point where she could be reasonable—even if that did confirm every last thing he'd said about redheads.

"Fine. If you don't want to work with the horse, there's lots of other things to be done, and I'm paying you for a full day. You can't be in very good shape if three hours of riding finishes you off, and I've always firmly believed that a rider has to be as much an athlete as his horse. Maybe with some work you can regain the suppleness and flexibility of your youth."

Dace's mouth had whitened into a line of anger. He strode across the ground between them. She tried to scramble away, but her hip was long past its tolerance and her leg folded underneath her.

Dace ignored her little mew of pain and humiliation, and caught her hard against his chest.

"You may pay me, you little witch, but you didn't buy me."

He tangled his hands in her hair and forced her chin up.

She swore to herself that she'd bite him if he had the audacity to try and kiss her. She swore it. And then his lips caught hers, and her vow was washed away by the unexpected ferocity of the storm that caught them in its grip.

Energy sizzled and hissed through her veins at the punishing touch of his lips, at their insolent insistence that she part her own lips and let his storm invade the cool cavern of her mouth. She wanted to pull away from him, or at the very least not to respond to him. But how could tinder not respond to a match? She was not thrusting him away, and not being passive either. She was meeting him, head-on, breath for heated breath.

Kissing him was like having her body invaded by a storm; sensations of hot and cold ripped through her, thunder invaded her heart, lightning bolted through her belly, and hot rain pelted the surface of her skin. She was awash with sensation. Tingling. Flying. Soaring. Diving.

Then, with stunning suddenness, the storm spent itself. He pulled away from her abruptly, and she stood, dazed, as if left drenched and unprotected after a real storm. She shivered, and Dace smiled coldly.

"The advantages of maturity, Princess," he said quietly. "See if any callow youth can make you feel like that."

It took every bit of energy she had left, but she drew herself to her full height, took the weight off her cane, and arched an eyebrow at him. "Like what?" she said coolly. Before he could respond she turned away. "Be at the pool at one-thirty, Mr. Stanton. A few laps a day will probably work wonders on that middle-aged pot."

She limped away. Though she didn't hesitate, she could feel herself cringe inside, waiting for the blow. She was sure he'd quit. And a part of her wanted just that. For him to quit. The utter and unforgivable audacity of the man! How could she be entirely professional about this training program if he was going to behave like a complete outlaw?

Quit, she begged him mentally.

But there was only silence from behind her. After she had walked a long way, she risked a glance back. Dace Stanton, masculine vanity etched into every handsome line of his face, was gazing at his flat belly with shattered disbelief.

CHAPTER FIVE

CADENCE had heard Dace show up at the pool at one-thirty. She did not go down—indeed could not, since she was lying on her bed so exhausted that she could barely move, never mind face him again. She thought he would just go away. Instead, after a while she heard the hard plop of a body hitting water, and then the steady swish of someone swimming laps.

There was a soft rap at her door a while later. Timothy's soft voice informed her that Lionel had arrived.

She felt an odd flatness, quite different from the little rush of *hope* she had felt every time Lionel had appeared since the accident. She debated seeing him, and decided she would, though for a moment it struck her as odd that she had the energy to handle one man, but not another, especially when it seemed that who she should be able to handle, and who she should not be, were inexplicably reversed.

She made Lionel wait. She certainly wasn't going to see the man who had rejected her without looking her most attractive. And, when she gave herself a final glance in the mirror, she was quite pleased with the results. Her hair looked wild and tangled, her cheeks sported high copper color, and her eyes glowed with a surprising light that no makeup bag could ever hope to accomplish. In fact, she noted with astonishment, she looked like a woman who had just got out of bed. Surely a look like that didn't come from one savage, stolen kiss? The thought brought even more color blazing to her cheeks. Of course it didn't. She was probably nearly feverish from her overexertion this morning.

She coupled her unexpectedly sexy appearance with a complete contrast—a soft white Angora sweater, of the most virginal white, and pleated white cotton trousers.

When she paused in the doorway to the sitting room, Lionel glanced up, and her efforts were rewarded. His jaw dropped, and unguarded desire burned through the pale blue of his eyes. Until the exact moment he saw her cane, and then what had been in his eyes was gone.

She greeted him coolly, and they talked about mutual acquaintances and horses for a while.

"Did you come for something in particular?" she finally asked. Surely Lionel had not always been this boring? It must just be the constraint of their history together that made him seem this way.

"I was kind of wondering what you were planning for Storm."

"Hmm," she said noncommittally. It occurred to her that she was not very surprised. He had already taken her staff, and now he was after her horses. She didn't even feel any fresh pain at his callousness. In fact she felt a little tickle of mischievousness. It might be quite fun to keep Lionel hanging for a month or two.

"I need to think about Storm a little bit," she said demurely. "Why don't you call me next week?"

She walked him out onto the porch and down the stairs, rather enjoying the discomfort her awk-

wardness caused him. Quite different from another
man, who'd known her all of two days when he'd
pronounced with utter and thoughtless sincerity that
he'd *forgotten* she had a handicap.

At that exact moment, out of the corner of her
eye, she saw Dace cutting through the hedge that
surrounded the pool.

Never mind that he'd forgotten she had a handicap. He was just a bloody forgetful man. Because
he'd also forgotten his manners, and forgotten who
the boss was! Well, this would stop him from
thinking he could just go about punishing whoever
he wanted with a kiss!

Without thinking she flung herself at Lionel,
coiled her arms around his neck, and kissed him
on the lips with all the pretended passion she could
muster.

And then nearly panicked when, instead of
pushing her away, Lionel responded with heat.

She broke away from him, and stared at him,
wide eyed. She was utterly confused by what she
saw in his face. He most certainly had not been
repulsed by her!

"What was that all about?" he asked, after a
long pause.

"Just an impulse," she said sheepishly.

"Ah," he said. "I'll call you next week, then."
He paused. "About Storm."

She stared at his departing back. "About Storm."
How could a man kiss you like that, and then try
to tell you he was only interested in your horse?

But then he wasn't the only guilty one, was he?
How could a woman kiss a man like that, just to
tell another man "hands off"? Her eyes flew to
Dace. She could only see his back. He was saun-

tering casually back to the stable. She suspected he was whistling carelessly.

She turned and stamped into the house, and slammed the door behind her.

She was not entirely surprised when Dace showed up for work the next morning. But she nearly went into shock at what he showed up *in*. He looked utterly male and utterly magnificent with the riding breeches molding every ripple of the muscle in those incredibly long legs.

Some feminine part of herself—a part that she would have dearly liked to kill—almost whimpered out loud at the sight that he made. She felt, with fresh agony, the ugliness of her handicap. She had intended to apologize, first thing, for her shrewishness yesterday. Now she found herself unable to do that.

"Life is full of surprises," she commented.

"Don't say one more word," he cautioned, his lips barely moving in a tightly haughty face.

She opened her mouth rebelliously.

"Not one, Cade."

There was no hint in his eyes, or his voice or his stance, that this was the selfsame man who had grabbed her and kissed the living daylights out of her yesterday.

Which was good. Wasn't it?

"Perhaps I was surprised that, after that *altercation* yesterday, you showed up at all."

"Oh, I suspected when I signed on that there might be an *altercation* or two," he drawled.

"Well, you had better not try and resolve any more of them with your lips!"

"You won't have to lose any sleep over that possibility," he assured her coldly.

"Humph," she said crisply. "We're going to work with that hammer-headed black gelding over there today. His name is Tim Mix..."

And then that other persona clicked in. The persona that had made her such a fierce competitor, the persona that allowed her to zero in on one thing, and think of nothing else at all. She became totally absorbed in the task of making him a top contender in the field of open show jumping.

He seemed as capable of zeroing in as she, for they progressed in tremendous strides that morning, despite yesterday's run-in. She began to see that he was a complete natural and that there was a very good possibility she could be entering him in shows by the end of the summer. It was a thrilling prospect, and it must have showed in her face that she was happy.

As Dace was taking the saddle from Tim Mix he slid her a look and grinned.

"I wore the riding breeches today because the blue jeans rubbed the skin right off my knee yesterday," he confessed gruffly. "And don't say 'I told you so' either."

She responded in the same light tone. "Do I look like the type who would say 'I told you so'?"

"Yes," he came back bluntly.

"I think I deserve that. Look, forget about the swimming. I was in a bad mood yesterday. I might have been trying to throw my weight around." It was very hard to say it.

"You might have been," he agreed, just a hint of a smile turning up the fine line of his mouth. "I took your order as an invitation. I like swimming."

She looked at the powerful sweep of his shoulders. It showed. She felt her face redden when he raised an eyebrow at her inspection.

"I didn't mean it about your stomach." She felt her face grow a few degrees hotter. But there was no sense doing things in halves.

"That wasn't the part that hurt," he said, his eyes unrelenting on the bright hotness of her cheeks.

"Oh?"

"The part that hurt was being called middle-aged. I don't think twenty-nine qualifies me for middle age, does it?"

"Are you only twenty-nine?"

"Thanks. Nothing like a little salt in the wound," he said dryly. He turned away from her, and fished through a grooming kit for a currycomb.

"It's not that you look older," she said hastily, studying his face, and realizing it was true. "It's that you act older. Er—more mature, I mean."

He began brushing the horse. "My dad died when I was seventeen. I had to quit school, and run a pretty big ranch. I guess I grew up fast. I guess it probably shows."

She felt as if he had just given her a little peek inside him. It was the first time he'd really said anything personal about himself, and she wondered if there was a small chance that some day they might get along. Respect and care for one another—in a purely professional sort of way, of course.

"I guess a lot of things age a man," he said quietly, almost to himself, and she glimpsed something she had glimpsed before in him—some terrible sadness. A tragedy that probably matched her own tragedy.

The feeling she had for him absolutely terrified
her. There was nothing professional about it. For
a shocking second she felt a strange, inexplicable
tenderness, a yearning to run her hands over his
weathered, world-weary face, and make him young
again, and carefree....

Instead, she turned away, quickly, afraid that her
raw emotion would be in her face, making her vulnerable, when that was the one thing she had sworn
she would never be again.

"Use the pool any time you want," she invited
gruffly, and then made her slow and painful way
back toward the house.

Dace had almost begun to think nobody lived in
that giant house. He'd swum every afternoon. No
one had ever come to those darkened windows. No
one had ever joined him in the pool.

Then, one day, after he'd been working for
Cadence Copperthorne for just about a week, he
had hauled himself out of the pool to see James
Copperthorne watching him—he suspected waiting
for him.

An interesting conversation had followed. A very
interesting conversation. The upshot of it had been
James Copperthorne handing him some video cas-
settes that he said might help him understand what
he was undertaking a little better. Dace was un-
certain whether Copperthorne had been referring
to the sport of jumping, his fiery daughter, or both.

He certainly wasn't about to pass on a chance to
understand Cadence Copperthorne. When she had
hired him, he had expressly understood he would
ride Storm Warrior, and yet that was the one horse
he had not yet ridden. And she was vague about

when he would get a chance at that magnificent animal, even though he pressed her on the subject.

Of course, she was mostly a witch. A bad-tempered, demanding, aggravating, self-centered witch, who must have put some kind of spell on him, because he couldn't get the taste of her damn mouth out of his mind.

And she managed not to be a witch when he was actually in the saddle. He couldn't help but be impressed with her knowledge, and the way she presented it. He actually didn't mind the instruction portion of being with her at all.

And, of course, there was the fact that every now and then her smile reached her eyes, and it was like the sun coming out from behind a cloud. And that was the look that had been on her face, he reminded himself grimly, after she'd kissed that guy on her front porch...

Dace raced to the fridge, and popped the cap off another Coke on his belt buckle just before he sat back down. His timing was perfect. The next segment was just beginning. He'd finally found the time to sift through the videocassettes James Copperthorne had given him. So far he'd watched five victory rides by Cadence and Storm. The part he liked the best was when she unsnapped the chinstrap of her helmet, jerked it from her head, impatiently took the ribbon from her hair, and raked her fingers through the hair of her braid. And then she gave that magnificent head of hair a shake, and it shimmered down around her shoulders, and swung around her face, and she looked at the camera, her eyes bold, and defiant and laughter-filled.

She and the horse were sheer poetry. There was
nothing else to describe it. He had never seen such
fluidity of movement, never seen such strength and
grace. He could barely tell that she controlled the
horse. They moved at each jump at what seemed
to be the same patient, controlled pace. But he knew
from the reading that he'd taken on in his spare
time that that wasn't quite the case—only that the
easier she made it look, the better she was at it, the
harder she had worked.

Twice he'd seen the blond guy kiss her after her
victories. The same one she had so soundly kissed
on her front porch. He didn't much like that. Not
because of Cade—why would he care who threw
themselves on her claws?—but because there was a
sneering superiority about the man that made him
instantly dislike him. Of course, he was pretty
certain that was the guy who had tossed her off as
though she were a broken doll after the accident,
and he didn't like it that the relationship did not
seem to be entirely resolved, though he wasn't even
sure why he didn't like it.

He settled in to watch the next video. This, he
promised himself, would be absolutely the last one,
before he turned in for the night. Of course, he'd
already made that promise to himself twice. But
somehow, watching these tapes, he was getting a
sense of excitement he hadn't had before. Given
time, he was going to ride like that. He would be
the one guiding that magnificent horse over those
awe-inspiring jumps.

On the video, Cadence swung the horse through
a sharp corner; he could see her barely perceptibly
shortening the big horse's stride for the final jump
of that round.

And then the world went crazy. The big horse was lifting—his takeoff perfect, Cadence up out of the saddle and leaning over his neck. And then, mid jump, it was as if the horse had been shot. He twisted violently sideways, came smashing down on top of the jump. She had been taken totally off guard—it was such a bizarre movement that nothing could have prepared her for it. She slipped sideways, and was right underneath the horse when his full weight smashed into the ground.

"Cadence!" The tortured scream ruptured the air, and the picture suddenly swung wildly, and then the camera came to rest, still filming, showing James Copperthorne racing toward his daughter. She was lying still, so still, a crumpled, lifeless heap on the ground, her body twisted at a preposterous angle. If he didn't know she was alive, Dace would have sworn she was dead. Chaos ensued, the camera recording blithely on. The far-off wail of sirens, several people chasing after the near maddened horse. And then a flicker of stripes and the dull hiss of dead air.

Dace rested his elbows on his knees and cradled his head in his hands. He felt limp and wrung out. His composure was completely gone. He took several deep, steadying breaths, and then, using the remote control, rewound the tape. Taking another deep breath, he took his thumb off the rewind, and watched the approach and takeoff again and again, and again. And then again.

Finally, aching with weariness, he went and switched off the TV. He rubbed his aching head. But, even lying in bed, he kept running the same few seconds of tape through his head, looking for the reason. And remained baffled that he could find nothing to account for the horse's behavior. Storm had been going beautifully, and then suddenly he had just gone completely mad. Or so it would seem.

"On his good days, he's very, very good," Cadence had said that day, paraphrasing some old nursery rhyme. "But on his bad days he's horrid."

He wondered, sadly, if she would ever again be the spirited, laughter-filled woman whom he had seen in those home videos. Not that she lacked spirit. But the mischievousness and the laughter seemed to have been lost. At least he knew, now, with the most reluctant of knowledge, why Sloan cared for her so much.

Cadence watched Dace narrowly. He was performing what was asked of him perfectly, but without heart. He seemed preoccupied today, as he had all week. She did not like the way he had started looking at her—with something haunted at the back of his eyes. She was having trouble placing where she had seen that look before, but it felt like an arrow piercing her heart.

He had been riding Storm since Monday. She didn't like that, either, though she wasn't sure why. She had no memory of her accident, or the day it had happened. Her doctor had told her that was a normal reaction to trauma, and also warned her that now and then some things would "twig" her memory. Unexpectedly, a picture might superimpose itself on her brain, or she might be nearly overwhelmed by a nameless anxiety, an edginess. She was certainly getting that feeling today. She tried, again, to shake it off.

Really, they were magnificent looking, there was no two ways around that. She knew she had made quite a picture on that horse once, too, but it was because of the contrast—her slightness against the brute strength and athletic ability of the horse. This was a better match. It was power. Pure power.

Storm was behaving beautifully for Dace, which should have helped her relax, but didn't. She felt as if she was waiting; waiting for the explosion, and every time the horse did something even slightly unexpected she jumped, and then tried to cover her fear and embarrassment by snapping and snarling at Dace. At least his eyes were losing that haunted look and just getting dark with anger, and he didn't seem to have a clue how fearfully hard her heart beat every time that big, beautiful horse danced sideways or snorted.

She glanced at the sky, and shivered. It was lead gray. The wind was picking up, and there was an occasional spit of rain.

"Dace, do the cavalletti again, at a trot." Her hip was sore. She felt deflated that he was working in such a lackluster fashion even though she knew her own brusque manner could at least be partly blamed.

"Did you hear me?" she called sharply.

Instead of obeying her order, he touched his heels to Storm's sides and began to trot wide, completely ignoring the cavalletti and the small jump at the end of the bars.

She stared at him incredulously. He must have misunderstood. She repeated her command.

Dace didn't even look at her. But he touched his heels to Storm's sides again, and they moved into an easy controlled canter.

She felt furious color boiling up under her skin.
The man was deliberately defying her. She screeched
at him to stop.

He ignored her.

"Dace Stanton, you stop it right now! That isn't
what you're supposed to be doing. This is——"

"Mutiny," he filled in for her, cantering by her
again. She felt as if she was going to start crying.
He was mocking her—mocking the fact that she
couldn't even step out in front of the horse and
make him stop. Mocking the fact that she was
crippled. He took the small jump at a canter.

"You aren't ready to be doing that——" she
yelled, impotent with fury, her knuckles white on
her cane.

He went by her again. Lord, he was magnificent.
He looked for all the world as if he'd been born
riding like this. Not ready for it? He looked as if
he was ready for anything her world of riding could
throw at him. Which, for some reason, increased
her fury.

"If you don't stop right now," she cried over the
steady rhythmic thudding of the hoofs, "I'm going
to dock you a week's salary. I mean it!"

He tossed her a coldly disdainful look over his
shoulder, and then wheeled the horse abruptly, and
galloped him straight across the school area.

She felt herself go white. He couldn't be! But he
was, unaware or uncaring that his stride was all off.
The horse was going at the fence far, far too fast.
They couldn't possibly——

Storm bunched up, too close to the fence, and
plopped over it. Dace lost his seat and was hanging
off one side, trying to right himself using Storm's

mane. He'd lost control and Storm wheeled around the corner of the stable and out of her view.

She stared after them with tears of anger and humiliation growing at the corners of her eyes.

She turned to walk away, suddenly aware of how terribly weary she was. She should never have let him take Storm yet. Maybe she should never have started this whole business. She was no match for that powerful pair.

Dace came around the corner, walking, leading Storm. He opened the gate and came in.

"I hope you fell off," she remarked viciously.

"I did," he said quietly.

"Do you know how much that horse is worth?"

"I'll assume it's something more than I make in a year," he answered indifferently.

"That was a foolish, irresponsible thing to do, and I meant it about the week's salary——"

"Fine," he said quietly. "You can have it deducted off my final check."

Her mouth fell open. "Your final check?" She forgot immediately that she had just been questioning the wisdom of this venture herself.

"You heard me."

"You're being childish," she said, but she could feel her mouth starting to tremble.

"Childish? From you? Now that's a laugh. I'll tell you what I'm being. I'm being man enough to decide I don't want to be some rich girl's toy any more. I don't know what's going on with you this week, but I don't particularly like being treated with less respect than you'd show your dog, Miss Copperthorne—like some robot that can be trained to go out and get you a few more silver trophies and blue ribbons to stuff in your tack room."

She stared at him. Oh, Lord, she had been
treating him just as he said. Giving him commands
as if he were a piece of wood rather than a human
being. But not for the reason he thought. Part of
it was the uncomfortable uneasiness being twigged
by the horse, some vulnerable place inside herself
that she didn't want anybody to see. But, even as
she acknowledged that, she knew that vulnerable
place went even deeper than she wanted to see. She
was also afraid of him. She was afraid that if she
treated him any other way—treated him like the
man she was so aware he was—he would *know*.

Know, somehow, that his eyes were the last ones
she thought of before bed; know, somehow, that
he entered her thoughts more than he ought. Know
that she dreamed the dreams of a normal, healthy
woman, even though she felt she no longer had a
right to such dreams. As if a healthy specimen of
a man like this would ever be seen dead with a
woman who limped so atrociously, who looked so
clumsy and awkward. His grace demanded a
complement that she would never be able to give
him.

She had to keep the boundaries clear, in her mind,
in her voice. She had to treat him the way she did—
coldly and impersonally. Because if she ever let her
guard down and showed him how attractive she was
coming to find him, he would probably die
laughing. Oh, not to her face, of course. To her
face, he would remain solemn and impartial, with
only pity coloring the blue of his eyes.

"I'm sorry," she said, her voice strained, "I certainly didn't mean to offend you. I may have been
a little curt——"

"A little curt?" he spat incredulously. "Lady, the jump instructors who push reluctant recruits out the doors of airplanes are more polite than you. Bank robbers with sawn-off shotguns show more grace in asking for what they want. Fevered boys in the back seats of cars show more finesse——"

"I think I get your point——" she said, struggling for composure.

He regarded her high color and pinched expression thoughtfully. "And a prude, besides."

"I am not!"

"Oh, come on. The mere mention of a back seat——"

"That was entirely inappropriate to this conversation! It was an extremely crude reference——"

"Okay. Okay. Please don't remind me, again, that I belong on the other side of the tracks. I think I've received that particular message loud and clear."

"I never said any such thing!" she protested.

"Not in words. I've got the message in every other way you can give it. You don't use my name. You don't say please. You don't say thank you. You don't say well done. As I said, I'm tired of being your toy. Find somebody else to help you paper the world in blue ribbons."

"Dace, I never knew I was making you feel that way. I——" She hesitated. What could she say? That she was so involved with her own feelings that she had stopped considering his? She didn't know when she'd become so selfish and self-involved, but it shocked her to be confronted with her own behavior.

She wasn't good at apologizing, though heaven knew she was getting enough practice at it around

Dace. But, even while the words were still formu-
lating in her head, he turned and walked away.

Her brief moment of illumination disappeared,
and she felt angry all over again. This man made
her angrier than any single person on earth had ever
done! Here she had been, about to apologize, make
herself totally vulnerable, and he wasn't even prepared to listen to her.

"Damn you to hell!" she shouted at his departing back. "How could you be so stupid?" she
screamed, when he failed to stop. "Do you think
I'd spend all this time and money for a few blue
ribbons? Do you think it was ever for blue ribbons?
I may not be able to walk very well, you cretin, but
I can dream, damn it. Not paltry, stingy, stupid,
little dreams. Big dreams."

He stopped, and turned slowly, looking back at
her, his dark, thick eyebrows raised quizzically.
"What for, then?"

She was aware suddenly that she was crying, that
the tears were slithering down her cheeks and
splashing off the end of her chin.

"It was for gold," she said, her voice breaking.
"I wanted a gold medal."

For a long time he stood silently, gazing at her.

"An Olympic gold medal?" he finally asked
softly.

She recognized suddenly that that disturbing look
was back in his eyes. The one that had been
bothering her all day.

And then she recognized where she had seen it,
and couldn't believe that she hadn't recognized it
before. It was the same look that lived in her
father's eyes when he looked at her.

She brushed a stern hand across her cheeks. "I seem to have some dust in my contact lenses," she croaked.

"You don't wear contact lenses," he said softly. He was moving toward her, slowly and gracefully, like a big wolf circling its prey. No, more like a big male wolf circling a female wolf——

She stopped the thought. It was ludicrous. It was ludicrous, but dammit, there was enough instinct in her to know that something was going on by the look in his eyes.

"How do you know I don't wear contacts?" she snapped, trying to forestall him.

He wouldn't dare kiss her again. He'd promised her that. He was a man of honor and he'd said that she didn't have to lose any sleep over the possibility of his kissing her ever again.

"I notice things," he confessed simply, without embarrassment or apology. "All men notice things. For instance, I know it's not just contact lenses that you don't wear."

She crossed her arms defensively over her chest, knowing exactly what he was talking about. "What are you talking about?" she demanded.

He didn't answer her. She had a funny feeling he'd abandoned that code of honor that he was so fond of. Because he was still coming at her, his stride purposeful, but not nearly as purposeful as the look in his eyes.

"I knew you weren't concentrating on your riding," she accused heatedly, backing awkwardly away from him, from the look in those eyes.

He stopped. A cold light burned through his face and his eyes. "As I said," he said wearily, "find yourself another toy, Miss Copperthorne." He turned away.

"Dace." She couldn't believe that tortured sound came from her. "Please don't go. Please don't walk away from here with the only dream I have left. Please." Her voice was barely a whisper. The tears were clogging her throat. "I looked at your eyes, too," she whispered, watching him through the blur of her tears, feeling another shuddering sob rack through her.

Impossibly he seemed to have heard her. He stopped, his whole back stiff. He turned and looked at her. "What did you say?"

"Nothing!" she denied, flinging her head contemptuously. How could she be such a weak ninny? Well, she would not put on any more of a performance for this man.

He was coming back toward her, not a curious wolf now, but all predator, aggressive, sure of himself. She mourned the day she could have turned and fled from him, as lithe as a deer. It was humiliating just to have to stand here, her damn anguish and heartbreak bald in her face. She looked down in a last desperate effort to keep this man from invading her soul.

He stopped an inch from her. She knew because the toes of his boots had edged into the ring of her downcast vision. He waited for her to look up, as he knew she must. For a long time she defied the electrical command that he was sending her.

Then slowly, slowly, her spine stiff with pride, her eyes flashing warning, she snapped her head up and looked him right in the eye.

"What do you want?"

"This."

He reached out that strong brown hand, but she was surprised by the gentleness with which he touched her. A single finger rested on her cheek, traced the line of a tear to her chin, and then gently nudged her chin upward.

With his finger still on her chin, he dipped his head, and his lips lightly traced hers, tasting her. A shock wave went through her, and she jolted back, and a pain shot through her hip. The pain brought fresh tears to her eyes—because it reminded her who she was, what she must limit her dreams to. Not to gloriously able-bodied men like this. No, Lionel had made it plain what a normal, virile man could handle and could not handle.

When she tried to wrench her head away from his softly plundering lips, his gentleness abruptly died. He wrapped one hand through the wild tangles of her hair, and the other went to the small of her back, forcing her toward him, and then pinning her against his hard, lean length.

Oh, Lord, he felt good. He felt warm and vibrant and alive. He felt so entirely male. So strong. He smelled good; he smelled of horses and leather and sweat. The physical contact shattered the walls she had been building around herself. She needed to be touched. Oh, Lord, she was starved to be touched. Until last week, since the accident she had allowed no one to touch her—a manifestation of the self-doubt Lionel had introduced to her world.

She had always been a rider first. Anything else had come second. Being a woman had come second. Being a daughter had come second. Being anything else had never occurred to her. And when that had been taken from her—when her primary identity had been violently and suddenly stripped from her—she had simply concluded she was nothing. That there was nothing left of her. A shell. A broken spirit.

But when Dace had kissed her that first time, she had become aware that there was a part of her she had not even known existed that lived. And wanted to live. That lived to be kissed by him again.

Just like this. With his breath stirring an answering breath of life within her, with the heat of his loins where he was pressed against her stirring an answering heat in her that mocked that passion she had felt when she rode. She had thought that was the height of what she could be—until he had teased her once with this. No, she had never felt anything that could even mildly approach this. Lionel's kisses had been pleasant, but not this.

This was the life force itself. Strong. Pure. Powerful. And in this split second she knew she lived, and that she was more than she had ever, ever given herself credit for being. In this split second it became so headily apparent to her that riding was what she had *done*, not who she was.

For a moment, she stood gloriously free, having found herself. And then she threw herself over the precipice of real passion and was lost again.

Oh, but not in a gray and lifeless place, without light, without color, without passion. No, she threw herself eagerly into the very eye of the storm.

He sensed the change in her, and answered it. He pressed her lips open with a tender, stern command from his teeth. His tongue invaded the warm hollow of her mouth, like drug into a vein. She felt ignited.

This was not the pleasant or languorous sensation of a warm sunny afternoon. This was storm. Vigorous. Exciting. Challenging. Wild. Beyond taming. And yet still a part of her rose to the challenge of it. She mounted the whirling storm of her passion and rode it.

Her tongue answered the quest of his, tangled with his, boldly explored his taste and his texture. He tasted good, his mouth sweet and smoky. Exotic sensation shivered up and down her spine and intensified as his fevered hands began to explore the satin of her skin. She had never been so aware of that surface of her body, of its ability to feel, to tingle, to tempt, to absorb sensation, to give.

Her own hands tugged at his shirt, until it pulled free of his jodhpurs. Her heated hands moved with hunger over the powerful corded muscle of his lower back, then slid around to the front of him, tracing the hard plane of his stomach. Steel sheathed in silk.

The storm had been brewing all day, and now it broke over them. A storm of fire erupted inside her, just as the storm outside them broke. Rain poured down in slashing sheets, though for a while they were so warmed by their own fires that they could ignore it.

She was dazed when his lips finally released hers, and she slumped against him. He gathered her in his arms, as if to protect her, as if he would never let her go. He was staring down at her with that disturbing, unfathomable look in his eyes. The look she had been seeing in his eyes all week.

She recognized it, and didn't want to believe it. But she knew. She knew. How could she have forgotten? How could she have let passion override the fact that Dace Stanton looked at her with a faint sadness, so remarkably like her father's, as if he knew what she once had been and wished it back?

She jerked away from him. And then she raised her hand and hit him across the cheek so hard it turned his head. Slowly, he turned back to her. It looked, for a moment, as if he might raise a hand to rub where the red welt was appearing on his cheek, but she suspected pride prevented him from allowing her to see she had succeeded in hurting him.

"I don't need your pity. Do you understand? And I don't need you to ride my horse. Quit if you want to. You were absolutely right— I'm just a rich girl who needed a new toy to play with." It was raining so hard he would have no way of knowing those were tears slithering down her cheeks.

"Lady," he said, with dangerous quiet, "nobody pities a wildcat."

He turned abruptly from her and went and took Storm by the reins, and urged him at a trot toward the stables.

Only once he was safely in the shadows did he look back at her. She was limping painfully. Every step looked like an exercise in anguish. Her nose was so high in the air that she might be drowned.

He touched his cheek where she had walloped him, and felt a cold anger with her. And with himself. What the hell did he think he'd been doing?

But he knew he'd been thinking of little else except plundering that wide mouth again since he'd seen that videotape. And he had no regrets. Lord, the woman was fire. Absolute fire. Not that he had any intention of getting burned.

Damn it, against his better judgment he wanted her to have that dream that she yearned for. That she had sacrificed herself for.

Maybe deep inside him he wondered if the dream could make her back into the woman who'd ridden Storm Warrior, the one who seemed to be full of easy laughter and mischievous eyes... Even a fraction of that woman was something to behold.

Lord, that kiss had held more lightning than the damn storm.

Storm Warrior was nervous inside the stable. He was always nervous inside. Dace picked up a handful of straw and began rubbing him down.

"Well, boy, what do you say? You want to go for the gold? You owe her, you know."

Dace didn't. He didn't owe her a bloody thing. But it seemed to him there were different kinds of gold in this life. And suddenly he wanted, just once, at any price, to see what a moment or two of happiness would do to the gold of her eyes.

What exactly did that sneering blond man mean to her?

"I don't care," he muttered to himself. But if he didn't care why did he think of her kissing *him* that day on the porch so much?

He sighed. Of course, he was in this anyway. He owed Sloan, and Sloan had called in his debt. He had too much of a sense of honor to back out now.

It was still mostly for Sloan, he told himself. He'd finish what he had started ... for Sloan.

He decided firmly that he'd sell his soul to the devil before he'd give in to the heavenly temptation of her lips again. He sighed. He hoped that after their discussion today she'd have the decency to start wearing a bra.

He grinned, well aware that he didn't hope that at all.

CHAPTER SIX

"OH," CADENCE said haughtily, the following Monday morning. "You didn't quit, after all."

It was a hazy day. A huge forest fire several hundred miles to the west had blanketed the whole region in smoke. The sun burned red behind a curtain of yellowish gray.

Dace turned from tightening Storm's girth, and gave her a measuring, slightly amused look. Though she would not have been able to come up with a shred of evidence to support her theory, she was fired with the certainty that somehow Dace Stanton *knew* she was wearing a bra today.

She wondered if he also knew she'd sat in the shade of the veranda on Saturday and Sunday, with binoculars trained on the stables. Originally, she'd just done it—admittedly with her heart in her throat—to see if he was packing to leave. And she'd been surprised to see he was out in the school, riding Ohmylady.

On Sunday morning he'd hauled old practice jumps out of storage, and with much consulting with a book he'd mapped out a course. In the afternoon, he'd saddled Storm, and for a moment she'd thought he had the audacity to start on the bigger jumps himself. But he had let himself out of the gate and disappeared to somewhere on the ranch . . . which had made her speculate uneasily if he was tired of being watched.

"Yes, ma'am. I think I can ride your Storm."

She started, then eyed him narrowly. Had that been a reference to that kiss that had passed between them? That *stormy*, electrical, unforgettable kiss? She decided to ignore his possible double meaning.

Besides, it probably wasn't a reference to the kiss at all. Storm seemed to be in one of his jittery moods today. Dace was saying he could handle the horse—nothing more.

"Yes," she said sharply, "I noticed you can ride Storm. You did quite a bit of it this weekend. You might have asked, you know."

He turned and gave her an undisturbed grin. He shook his head slightly. "You looking for a fight this morning, Cade?"

"Certainly not!"

"Then why don't you thank me for showing dedication and ambition far beyond the call of duty! I was riding these horses and setting up the jumps on my own time, after all."

"It's not that I don't appreciate it," she said with stubborn coolness, "it's just that it might have been nice to have been consulted."

Dace shook his head again. "That still didn't sound much like a thank-you."

She felt backed right into a corner. He had a point. He was giving her something she couldn't begin to pay him for: his enthusiasm. His utter involvement in what they were doing. His willingness to immerse himself in this new world.

"Thank you," she snapped. "There. Are you happy now?"

"Sure," he said evenly. He vaulted into the saddle and looked down at her. "Are you?"

"You might have asked. That's all."

"Cade Copperthorne, a man wouldn't want to give you too much rope. Before I knew it I'd be asking for permission to take off my boots at night. I took some initiative. That's a *good* thing."

"Are you implying that I'm bossy and domineering?"

"No, ma'am. Just a pretty typical redhead."

"You seem to know more about redheads than the *Encyclopaedia Brittanica*," she said scathingly.

He grinned again. "And learning a little bit more every day." Storm skittered sideways unexpectedly. "Hey, buddy, none of that," Dace said, completely unruffled. His voice was stern and calm.

Cadence had felt just one of those feelings the doctor had warned her about. A phantom fear had stabbed through her like a knife.

"Storm might not be the best choice for today and I don't know about those jumps. I don't know if you're ready for them." Actually, she knew damn well he was ready for them, but she wanted to reassert who was the boss... and hide the twinges of fear behind a wall of aggression.

"Look, Cade, I've been doing quite a lot of reading, and you're going to ruin your horses taking them over jumps so much smaller than what they're capable of."

His tone was reasonable and she knew he was right.

Dace turned the horse away toward the school. Cadence knew that if the dream was ever going to become a reality the moods of the horse could not be pandered to. Still, she felt herself trying to remember if Storm had given her warning signals like this the day of the accident. She couldn't remember.

She became aware that Dace had stopped and was watching her, a frown on his face. "Are you coming?"

A leaf rattled by Storm and the horse stiffened and sidled sideways, toward her. She did not want to be around this powerful horse today. His edginess, his leashed power, were stirring up something within her. She hoped her disturbed ghosts were not evident in her face. She did not want to be vulnerable in front of Dace.

"Not today," she said shakily. "I just came to tell you I don't feel well. If you wanted to do some more hacking today——"

"Hacking?"

"Trail riding. I——"

Comprehension dawned in his eyes. "The horse is making you nervous, isn't he?"

She watched Dace, unable to speak. She searched his face for the mockery she dreaded, but did not find it there. She found something worse: compassion. That look again. That look that asked her to be something she no longer was. But he had never known her before. How could he possibly be looking at her like that? With that look that was so similar to the one she saw on her father's face? On Timothy's?

No, that wasn't quite true. There was a dimension more to the look he gave her. A dimension one did not find on one's father's face—ever. It reminded her of their last stormy kiss, and the fear in her increased. She did not feel bold today. Nor passionate.

"The phone's ringing," she announced with relief. Her calls from the house could be put through to the phone in the tack room.

Dace cocked his head. "So?"

"So, I'm expecting a call . . . from Lionel!" She
didn't know if the name Lionel meant anything to
Dace, but she noticed that, lately, whenever she was
feeling vulnerable she felt she needed a shield to
throw up in front of her. Lionel, she thought with
a trace of wryness, was a bit of a paper shield. A
name with nothing behind it.

Dace's face was bland and his tone dry. "By all
means, go talk to your boyfriend."

As it turned out, it *was* Lionel on the phone. He
made her very angry by offering outright to buy
Storm and then offering her a ridiculously low
figure because the horse was a "renegade."

By the time she went back outside the phantom
fear had vanished—seemed as ridiculous as Lionel
calling her magnificent horse a renegade. Though
she didn't know it, her eyes were spitting sparks
that could well have been mistaken for passion.

"That's better," Dace said, eyeing her wryly. He
hesitated. "That fear will destroy you, if you let it.
It will keep growing and your world will get smaller
and smaller and smaller to accommodate its vo-
racious appetite. You're not really afraid of your
horse. You should figure out where that fear is
coming from."

She did not like the way he was looking at her,
his gaze steady and stripping, as though he could
see her soul. He seemed oblivious to the fact that
the horse was so uneasy underneath him.

"If I want a psychiatric evaluation," she informed him chillily, "I'll go for therapy. As it
happens Storm was edgy the day of our accident,
and it still makes me a bit nervous."

"He wasn't anything at all like this the day of your accident," Dace informed her softly.

She felt herself freeze, and she remained frozen while Dace slid out of the saddle, and stood in front of her.

"How do you know?" she whispered, both angry and dismayed.

"He was calm that day. He was going beautifully. You could have handled him even if he was acting up. He went crazy over one of the jumps, Cadence. No one could have stopped it. Nothing could have prevented it."

"How do you know?" she whispered accusingly.

"Can't you remember what really happened?"

He'd ignored her question. She wanted to persist but his voice, soft and insistent, had acted as a trigger. A scene flashed through her mind with vivid clarity. It had been a bright, beautiful day. Blue, cloudless skies. And Storm had been performing to the best of his potential. Not at all like today.

"You're right," she admitted slowly, "he wasn't restless. In fact, it was one of his better days. But that accident and its aftermath have left a sensitive part inside me, and sometimes..." she nodded toward the horse, "...he touches it. The doctor said it was normal."

Dace nodded. "I suppose it is. It won't last forever. You were a magnificent horsewoman. It wouldn't be natural for someone who spent as much time around horses as you did, who rode as well as you did, to be afraid of a horse."

"How do you know what kind of horsewoman I was?"

"I saw you around from time to time," he said carelessly.

She scanned his face, knowing that was probably true. Hacking was excellent conditioning for her horses and she'd ridden every inch of this property. Still, she sensed more, but also sensed he was not going to volunteer it. Or allow it to be prised out of him.

She turned suddenly away from him, despising both her weakness and his intuition. "I don't like being reminded of what I was," she informed him coldly.

He nodded. "So be angry, Princess. Be bloody angry at the hand life gave you to play. It's a bad one, and you have a right. But you remember something—good anger always feels clean. It'll give you the energy you need to get on with your life. Bitterness is something else. It'll just kill you slowly."

"How dare you call me Princess? If you don't mind your manners, I'll——"

"Now," he said smoothly, turning from her, and lithely leaping back into the saddle, "all you have to do is start directing that at the right source." He gave her a long, hard look that left her fuming and wordless, then turned again toward the riding school.

"Are you coming?" he threw the final challenge over his shoulder.

"I wouldn't miss it for the world," she snapped. "The way that horse is feeling today, you'll probably break your fool neck."

The session did not go very well. Dace had to fight Storm to get him to obey, but Cade realized she was not afraid. She had ridden Storm herself on days like this. It had never been pleasant, but it had not been particularly frightening either. Besides, it gave her a very good idea of how well Dace was riding that he handled the horse's edgy stubbornness with determination and ease.

But his words kept her awake very late that night. Dace perceived her as angry and bitter, which was not very flattering; even less flattering because she knew there was a grain of truth in it. What did he mean about directing her anger at the right source? Where was that?

She finally slept, but fitfully. She awoke to a dream of Lionel kissing her with raw and arousing passion. The dream was so real that she licked her lips to see if his taste really lingered. As with most dreams, there were a few details that didn't quite fit. Lionel, for instance, had been wearing Dace's cowboy hat.

Still, she felt the ache of loneliness his leaving her had left somewhere in the region of her heart.

Surely I'm not fool enough to still care about him? she asked herself. And she knew she was very close to knowing what she had always known: the anger and bitterness Dace had spotted were not directed at Storm. The horse had not hurt her out of malice. It had been an accident, and, as far as that went, how could one be angry at an accident? Life dealt the hands, and being angry about the cards wouldn't change them.

She limped. But she lived. Her mind drifted to her telephone conversation with Lionel that day, and she knew from the sudden stirring of rage within her that she had finally arrived at the place she sought.

Lionel. All this time, she had tried to suppress that rage. Tried to tell herself that Lionel had a right to feel the way he did, to walk away from

damaged goods. She had tried to understand his
point of view and in doing that she had ignored
her own right to have feelings. Maybe she had
hoped if she was kind enough and understanding
enough and brave enough Lionel would see her
virtue and come back despite everything.

That was foolish and naive. She was angry, and
Dace was correct—she had every right to be angry.
The man she thought she loved had behaved like a
shallow and despicable cad. In the end, she had to
acknowledge, she felt horribly angry at Lionel—
but also at herself. She was a fool. Not because she
still cared, because she didn't. But because she had
ever cared about a man like that. What did it say
for her that she had never seen what he really was?
That she had actually been so weak as to want him
back after the way he behaved?

She noticed a sudden cool breeze blow through
her window, and felt the heaviness lift from her.
The air, blessedly, was not smoke scented or hot.
She rushed to her window. It was still deepest night,
but the haze had cleared and the moon was shining.
The fresh air was irresistible.

She pulled jeans over her bare legs, and tossed
a light sweater over her shoulders and went down
the stairs into the night. She was drawn to the
stables. She didn't know why. She came around the
corner of the stable and then shrank back.

Storm and Dace stood together, washed silver by
the moon. She took in a long, shuddering breath.
Dace's forehead was pressed into Storm's muzzle,
and the horse and man stood absolutely stock-still,
frozen by the moon in a moment of unbelievable
communion.

She could hear his voice now, soft as velvet, soothing as the night itself.

"You were hurt, weren't you, big guy? I could feel it in you today. Some giant hurt coiled in you like a rattler. I wish you could tell me what it was. I wish you could."

Dace rolled away from Storm's head, leaned his back on those powerful withers. The horse reached around and nuzzled his cheek as Dace looked up at the stars.

"Me too, big guy. I guess that's why I like you so much. I can feel the sameness in us. A big hurt, where our hearts used to be, that never quite goes away."

Cadence stood in the shadows in shocked silence. She wanted to slip away, unseen. She knew that would be the decent thing to do. And yet, she did not. She moved out of the shadows, and crossed over to them, the moonlight streaming over them all.

Storm greeted her with a soft nicker, and Dace stiffened.

"It's me," she announced softly and slid her arms around Storm's neck. She regarded Dace over Storm's neck. "I couldn't sleep."

"Me neither." His eyes were hooded. "You shouldn't be wandering around in your pyjamas in the middle of the night."

She glanced down. Her sweater was open over the soft, transparent white of her teddy. She registered the fact that Dace was trying to embarrass her, that he didn't like being discovered at his most vulnerable.

She laughed softly. "Well, it's not as if I'm walking down a street in New York in the middle of the night, is it? I wasn't expecting to see anyone. Besides, Dace, I suspect you've seen women in their pyjamas once or twice before.''

With a total lack of urgency she pulled the sweater shut and crossed her arms over it. She eyed him solemnly.

"You know," she finally said slowly and softly, "I realize that sometimes I act as if, because the whole world can see my handicap, I'm the only one wounded. But I'm not, am I?''

His face looked remote, the silver of the moonlight giving it a granite cast. His eyes glanced off her face, hard and hooded. "No."

She took a deep breath, and plunged on, despite his lack of invitation. "I'd listen if you wanted to talk.''

"Thanks, Cade. Not tonight.''

She felt shut out. Rejected. But then what had she ever done to earn Dace's trust or respect? She made a move to leave and was surprised by the restraining hand on her arm.

"Don't go.''

She looked at him with question. His voice had been husky, faintly imploring. As if he too, at some point this night, had wrestled with the ghosts of loneliness.

"We need moments like this, you and I. Quiet moments, filled with dark skies and stars. A resting time.''

"Between battles?'' she offered wryly. But she was glad he wanted her to stay here with him, sharing the night. It took some of the sting out of his earlier refusal to let her into his private world. He wouldn't give her his past, but perhaps it meant something that he would want to share a small piece of the present, this moment, with her.

He smiled, his teeth white through the darkness. The guarded look had relaxed in his face. "Something like that."

"Redheads aren't terrifically good at being quiet," she informed him lightly, but then she let the silence wrap itself around her, and allowed herself to feel something she rarely felt in Dace's company: tranquillity. Comfort. Peace. He was right. They did need moments like this.

After a long time, she shivered regretfully. "I'm starting to feel chilly. I think I'll go in now."

"Wait. I want to show you something." She heard the hesitation in his voice even though his movements were a study in casualness as he picked up a stick that lay on the ground. He stepped slightly away from Storm and into a pool of moonlit dust.

She moved over beside him.

He was doodling in the dust. He glanced up at her. "How's that for surprising?"

DACE.

CADE.

His name written above hers in the dust.

"Do you see it?" he asked softly.

She shook her head, bewildered.

"The same letters," he pointed out. "The same ingredients, only mixed up differently. I thought it was strange, that's all. A weird coincidence, if you believe in them."

He had pushed her away tonight when he'd felt vulnerable, but now she could feel the blue of his eyes invading her when she felt vulnerable. That look was in his eyes again. The look she hated.

"Don't look at me like that," she ordered crossly.
"Like what?"

"It's the way my father looks at me, as if he wants
me to be what I once was."

He was silent for a time. "I guess that is what I
want, too," he admitted softly.

"You don't even know what I once was."

"Your father gave me some of the videos he made
of you riding."

She felt the blood drain from her face. She
clenched her fists. "You son of a bitch! How dare
you?"

The truce, that most pleasant interlude between
battles, came to a crashing end.

He was meeting her anger levelly. "I don't see
anything wrong with looking at them. In fact, I
thought you'd approve."

"Approve? Approve of you spying on me?"

"I didn't feel as if I was spying." He actually
smiled. "Spying implies all kinds of intrigue. All I
felt I was doing was learning in a brand-new way.
A good way." He hesitated. "It wasn't unpleasant
watching a beautiful woman ride her horse, but I
sure as hell didn't feel like a Peeping Tom." He
must have seen the expression in her face and read
it accurately. "You *are* a beautiful woman. You
don't believe that has changed, do you?"

"I'm not her any more," she said, her face absolutely frozen. "Why can't you all see that? Why
can't anybody just care about me the way I am
now? This instant?"

"Cadence," he looked stricken, "I was saying
that I didn't care about you now——"

"Don't call me that! Don't ever call me that
again!" It wasn't the first time the long version of

her name had slipped off his lips. But before she had enjoyed the sound of her name coming off his lips just enough to ignore the slip. Not now.

"It's your name," he said, his voice as uncompromising as steel.

"It's *her* name!"

"Don't say that as though a part of you is dead."

"A part of me *is* dead. The part you all want back. The Cadence who rode horses and walked courses and danced till dawn and ran through meadows with flowers in her hair..."

"That's not the part anybody misses. It's got nothing to do with your damn legs. It's the light in your eyes——"

"I told you before that I don't want your pity." She could hear the shrill wildness in her tone. "That's what this is all about, isn't it? A game. See if you can give me back my confidence. Give the poor, ugly cripple a real treat. Give her a kiss every now and then. I wouldn't be surprised if my father set you up——"

"Stop it. I told *you* once before that nobody feels any pity for a wildcat. You're a self-pitying little witch, and I wouldn't kiss you for your father's entire fortune."

And, having said that, he took her in his arms and bestowed on her the most punishing kiss of her entire life. His lips were bruising on hers. He plundered her mouth, stealing her very breath from her.

She willed herself to give nothing back to him, despite the white-hot heat uncoiling within her. Her willpower had nearly spent itself, her ache overcoming her anger, when suddenly he stepped back from her. It was obvious he was furious at his own lack of control as well as furious with her.

They stood eyeing each other, silently, warily. His shoulders were heaving. She was trembling.

"I can't make love like a normal woman," she told him, her voice tight with frozen control. "I can't have babies like a normal woman."

The anger was gone instantly from his face. He stepped toward her.

"Oh, Cadence," he said softly, his voice rough around the edges. His eyes were awash with feeling, denim blue in their intensity. "Oh, Cadence."

Her tone was hard, and her eyes glittered hard, too. "So tell me that isn't pity I hear now, Dace Stanton," she challenged coldly.

He said nothing.

She turned and stamped away, never more aware of the eyes that watched her.

CHAPTER SEVEN

"THERE'S a small but very well-respected show in three weeks," Cadence told Dace. "I think if we worked really hard——"

"I think we'd better talk about what happened last night," Dace cut her off smoothly.

"I am never going to talk about that," she stated with a cold finality that she hoped hid her intense embarrassment. She'd blurted out the most personal details of her life to this man! She'd acted as though he'd asked her to marry him when all he'd done was stolen a kiss on a moonlit night. He hadn't even kissed her out of passion. He'd been furiously angry.

The only way she knew to handle her acute embarrassment was to try and outrun it—by working them both nearly to death, if need be. Besides, maybe a common goal could divert this powerful electricity that leapt between them, channel it in a different—and safer—direction.

Dace was looking at her, shaking his head.

"How do you feel about ties?"

"Ties?" he asked, baffled.

"Well, we had some problems with the breeches. I'm just wondering if I'm going to have to hire a team of wrestlers to get you into a tie on show day."

Dace's fingers moved to his throat as though he were being strangled. "I don't wear ties," he told her grimly.

And she knew, mercifully, that the incident last night had been shelved. She felt her feet were comfortably back on solid ground when they spent the rest of the morning arguing amicably about ties and wrestlers.

It was a world she had missed, she thought poignantly, moving through the show grounds and sniffing the air. It smelled of horses and hay, and newly turned turf, and excitement. She'd forgotten how much energy and magic were at these smaller prize-money shows. This one was a Five—a good place to start Dace, though she hoped he would move quickly to Ones and One-As. A fist tightened in her stomach at the sheer audacity of her ambition, and she glanced around for Dace.

She had seconded her father's private plane and pilot to come. Though the show was only a few hours from home, a few hours in a car could be murder on her hip, and she was determined that all her focus was going to be on Dace, and her horses.

Dace had insisted on traveling the day before, with the horses, even though she had told him she preferred that he arrive fresh, too. She had been given a crisp lecture on a cowboy's code of honor, meaning a *man* looked after his own mount, and that had been that. She sighed. Dace was a very hard man to be a boss around. Ha. As if she had ever been his boss. The man was impossible, untamable, difficult...

Wonderful, a renegade voice inside her whispered, as she caught sight of him striding toward her.

"Thank heaven you're here," he said without preamble, tugging her into the shadow of a snack tent. "Where the hell have you been?"

A tiny part of her managed to voice the fact that it found this kind of greeting severely disappointing, even while another part panicked. "Is something wrong? Is Storm——?"

"Storm is fine. Would you look at this?"

He moved nearly on top of her and his scent filled her nostrils. But before she could be entirely swept away by his closeness a very lumpy tie knot was shoved in her face.

She stared at it, and bit hard on the side of her cheek. A chuckle escaped anyway.

"This is not funny," he proclaimed warningly.

"Of...course...not," she gasped.

"I've only worn a tie twice in my life. I just spent half an hour in a cold sweat trying to get this thing done up. Cadence, if you don't quit laughing——"

"I...am...not...laughing. I'm...I'm...listening."

"I couldn't ask one of these snobs to show me how to do it, and you're late!"

"I'm not late," she tried to defend herself.

"I don't need stuff like this," he muttered. "I've got four thousand things on my mind. I don't need this." He yanked impatiently on the tie.

She intervened before he strangled himself. "Now, Dace," she soothed. "I'll fix it. Relax. Relax."

And she could sense the tension leaving those big shoulders as she patiently undid the knot and retied it, slid it up snugly into the hollow of his throat, and folded his collar down. There was an intoxicating intimacy about it all, especially when she looked up to see those near-indigo eyes resting on her with a welcome that he had not given her in words.

She backed away from him. "The horses weathered the trip all right?"

"Beautifully," he murmured, but his eyes were still fastened to her face, and she had the confused notion that he wasn't talking about the horses.

"Have they drawn for order yet?" she said, trying to break the spell of his eyes.

It worked. He looked at his watch. "I have to go walk the course. Ohmylady drew third; Storm is near the middle of the class." He grinned. "Thirteen. Do you suppose that means anything?"

"No. How are your nerves, Dace?"

"Like steel," he said, and then leaned very close, so close that his breath stirred her hair. "I've never been more scared in my life."

His eyes held a wickedly mischievous light at that statement, but she felt suddenly afraid herself. Afraid because she had this silly impulse to stand up on her tiptoes and kiss him on the cheek.

He took her elbow and turned her toward the stable.

"Now, Dace, try to remember not to plop Storm over the fences. He has that longer stride, and——"

"There's no sense cramming the morning of the exam," he told her. "If I don't know it by now, it's too late."

"It was just a helpful reminder!"

"Well, it wasn't helpful."

She glared at him, and he gave her one of his absolutely charming lopsided grins.

"I get very wary when you use words like 'helpful,' Cade."

"Dace, you are not being very cooperative. This is the time we should be cementing our working relationship——"

"You are the last person I would trust cement to. The next thing I knew, my feet would probably be encased in the stuff."

"You're trying to distract me, aren't you, Dace?" she guessed suddenly.

"Distract you?" he said innocently. "Naw. Though I do hope that nervous energy coming off of you in waves isn't infectious."

"As a matter of fact, I'm not nervous!" She grinned ruefully. "Well, maybe a little. I was just looking for a way...to belong."

Dace stopped and looked down at her, his face totally solemn. He reached out, ran a large hand over the back of her head and then cupped her chin in his hand. "You belong here, Cade Copperthorne. You couldn't have taught me with such utter and compelling confidence if this weren't absolutely your world." His hand moved from her chin.

She felt her lip tremble slightly. "Thanks, Dace."

He nodded, and glanced at his watch. "You have a job to do today, and don't forget it. You know these horses. You know me. You know this world. And I'm counting on your ability to critique what we're doing out there to get us one step closer to that medal you want so badly. We're a team." He smiled. "But still no cement. Absolutely no cement."

She laughed out loud and felt some of the tension dissolve within her. Damn this man if he didn't have

a way of turning things around. Shouldn't she be
the one doing the pep talk? "Oh, go to work."

"You, too," he said softly.

He left her at the fence surrounding the course.
She looked it over. It was nicely done and not overly
complicated. She watched Dace walking it, and was
pleased by the concentration on his face, pleased
by the fact that he paced the water jump and the
following combination jump three times before he
was satisfied.

She was also—secretly—pleased with how he
looked. With the long hard line of his leg, with the
wideness of his shoulders beneath the black jacket.
His hair curled and sparkled under the sun, and
she knew he would wait until the very last minute
to put on the black hunt cap that he despised. She
realized she was looking at him with a kind of pos-
sessive pride, and was embarrassed by it. She wasn't
his girlfriend, after all. She looked studiously away
from him, afraid people might see her staring at
him, and see something beyond professional interest
in her gaze. And feel sorry for her for being ridiculous enough to yearn after such a gloriously able-
bodied man.

Suddenly, she stiffened. Lionel had appeared out
of the stable area and was walking right toward her.

She watched him, surprised by her detachment.
Once, sighting him would have been followed by
strong emotions, and the downward plunge of her
heart. Once, she would have felt the humiliating,
helpless pain of having lost him. Instead she felt
remarkably little, and what she did feel didn't feel
like love.

For the first time she noticed his handsome features had sharp edges, that he was thin and pale.

His face had a scowling superiority in its cast that she had never noticed before. He looked impatient and she remembered how hard he had been to please. Even when she'd gone perfect, he'd seemed to delight, not in constructive criticism, but in shredding her performance.

She wondered why she was seeing him in this light, but in the back of her mind she knew it was because she was comparing him to Dace. She wondered what right she had to compare him to Dace. Her relationships with the two men were completely different. And yet she compared anyway. Her eyes moved to Dace and she was oddly reassured by his nearness, by his strength, the healthy bronze of his skin, the gentleness she knew could be found in his eyes when it was needed.

Lionel saw her suddenly. For a moment the struggle was evident in his face. He wanted to pretend he hadn't seen her. Then he smiled, lifted a hand, and joined her at the fence, hooking one booted foot through the lower rung. "Wonderful to see you. I hardly knew that it was you," he rushed on, when she only nodded curtly at his effusive greeting. "I didn't expect to see you at this size of show."

"Or I you," she said bluntly.

"I've got a new mount," he said, looking over her shoulder, instead of into her eyes.

She said nothing. She turned back to the fence and watched Dace.

"Was that Storm Warrior I saw in the stable area?"

"Yes."

"Have you found someone interested in buying him? Are they giving him a try here? I've been thinking about my offer and——"

"And it was ridiculous," she cut him off coolly. "My horse is not for sale, Lionel."

"You've found a rider for him, then?"

She nodded, and Lionel's gaze followed hers out to Dace. His eyes narrowed and he looked back to her, an expression of unsettling knowing in his eyes.

Her worst fear was confirmed. Something of her strong feelings for Dace must be in her face.

"The horse was always too strong for you," Lionel said, with a certain satisfaction.

She stared at him, feeling disbelief at the bluntness of the blow. What he was really saying was that she was responsible for her own fate—that she had been riding way above her ability.

Startled, she realized she had unquestioningly accepted that explanation for the accident all this time.

But now she heard another voice, Dace's voice, telling her she'd ridden magnificently. And she trusted Dace. Not a single word ever came out of his mouth that he didn't believe to the bottom of his boots. And he would *know*. He knew horses and he knew Storm, and if he said she had ridden well that was a fact, not an opinion.

The conflicting views left her momentarily confused, but as she studied Lionel she tried to piece together the puzzle. Yes, she had ridden Storm well. It was true they had had one or two bad days, but nothing to suggest the outcome being as it was.

And then the memory she was seeking tickled the back of her mind. Of Lionel mounting Storm, just once, to demonstrate an approach to a jump. He'd made his point but he had not ridden the big horse well, and he had not attempted it ever again.

She watched him narrowly now. And saw what she had never seen.

"That horse and I were perfect together," she said with utter and cool confidence. "Why don't you admit it, Lionel? He would have been too strong for *you*. You couldn't have stood it if I knew the truth. I was a better rider than you."

Lionel's pale complexion took on a slightly mottled look. "I never denied you had talent. I was your coach. I wouldn't have taken you on if I didn't believe in you, and I was taking you to the top."

She shook her head. "I think I was getting to the top in spite of your coaching, Lionel, not because of it."

"How can you say such a thing? You loved me. We . . ." His voice trailed away uncomfortably.

She actually laughed. "How good of you to remember that. We didn't love each other, Lionel. You wouldn't have ditched me quite so quickly if you really loved me. You know, you behaved despicably. And walking with a limp for the rest of my life is a small price to pay for having been saved from a life with someone as superficial as you."

Lionel let his pale gaze drift meaningfully back to Dace. "I'm glad you feel it was worth it," he said slowly, his voice syrupy with sympathy. "There are so many things you will never have now."

She felt the cold shock of it. She knew exactly what he was saying: not to set her sights on a man like Dace. Well, she already knew that, and she sure as hell wasn't going to let him see he'd managed to hit her again where it hurt the worst.

"Such as what, Lionel?" she demanded, her voice glacial and her features schooled into a faintly amused mask.

"Well, the whole Olympic dream, of course," he said regretfully.

She knew that wasn't what he had been referring to at all, moments ago, but she'd take him at face value. "My stables are going to have a gold medal, Lionel. Maybe several of them before I'm done."

"And I'm not?" he asked grimly.

She shrugged. "Who knows, Lionel? You've got the best staff in the country at your stable now. But you don't have an eye for greatness in horseflesh. And you don't have a rider with that kind of potential, either."

He looked white and furious, though she was sure it was no surprise to him to be told that he didn't have the talent. Still, she shivered at the look of malice in his eyes, before he turned and walked away. She had just made an enemy. Out of a man who had once loved her.

No, that was not true. If he had ever loved her, he would not be able to hate her so easily, he would not be so intent on hurting her. What was it with Lionel, anyway?

Lord, she thought whimsically, she'd been a girl when she first met him. A little girl who'd fallen in love with her coach, as all little girls did, and then never taken a grown-up look at him when the time came.

The competition began a few minutes later, and Cadence watched critically as the first two horses completed the course. She knew well before either horse knocked down a fence that they were not contenders.

Dace was announced and he came out. If he was nervous now it didn't show at all. Ohmylady's ears were pricked forward, and she pranced slightly with excitement. Dace checked her easily. The whistle blew, and they began the course. The fact that they were both nervous showed only in the fact that they rushed the first two jumps. Then they seemed to settle into the task at hand, looking smoother and more relaxed with each jump. They rapped a pole on the combination jump, but it didn't go down. But it seemed to throw their timing slightly, and Ohmylady's takeoff was too close to the next fence. They knocked down the top bar. They recovered and went the rest of the course without fault.

Cadence was thrilled. Dace had done extremely well for his first time out. And four faults might not knock him out of the running.

Indeed, the next six horses also all received faults. Lionel was riding in the tenth position. And went clear.

Cadence tried to tell herself it didn't matter. That this was Dace's first show, and basically all they wanted to do was chalk it up to experience. And yet, there was a fierce competitor inside her, and a vengeful woman, too. A part of her wanted, impossibly, for Dace to win. And the victory would have been made even sweeter if it was over Lionel.

She tried to keep her expectations in check, but as soon as she saw Dace enter the arena on Storm Warrior her hopes soared again, unfettered.

What she saw pleased her immensely. Dace had looked good on Ohmylady. Now, teamed with the more powerful mount, and with his first-time-out nerves behind him, he looked electrifying. And he and Storm Warrior gave an absolutely electrifying performance. Though their round was not without flaw, the bold heart of the horse, and the iron determination of the man who rode him, more than compensated for the fact that they approached more than one jump too quickly or too closely.

They had a clear round and they finished, not to thunderous applause, but to startled silence. The horse was known, but Dace was a complete novice and he had taken spectators and competitors alike by surprise. The silence ended and the applause was deafening.

Cadence felt tears prick her eyes. Her heart was flying. She had been right. That very first time she'd seen Dace, racing the wind across rough fields, she'd been right. Her heart had recognized him, and it had been right. They were going to the top— he and Storm Warrior. There was nothing left of her envy that someone else would ride her dream. Watching them together had filled her with an awe that erased all else. Even though she'd been watching them practice, and they'd been good, they were even better at the show. They had that extra electrifying spark that born competitors brought to competition.

Two more horses in the field went clear, and there was a jump-off. Dace and Storm went clear, but their time placed them second. Lionel came fourth. As a bonus, Ohmylady ended up placing a respectable seventh in the competition.

She had lunch with Dace in the competitors' canteen, and was so excited she could barely swallow her hamburger. She happily went over the high and low points of the entire morning. She realized part of her babbling was pure exhaustion, and suddenly the words dried up and she practically slumped on the table.

"I think I'm going to cry," she informed him. "I'm so tired and happy."

"And your hip hurts," he guessed. "Cade, why on earth didn't you sit down? Every time I saw you, you were hugging the fence."

Tears did smart her eyes then. "I just forgot. I got so excited, and so wrapped up in the action, I just forgot. Can you imagine how wonderful that is for me?"

"Humph. You seem to *forget* quite often—to the point of abusing your hip. Sometimes lately I wonder if it's not getting worse——"

It seemed to her this was just underlining Lionel's observation of this morning. She didn't want Dace to notice her injury. She didn't want his advice or his sympathy. If he wasn't going to give her the kind of attention he'd give any red-blooded woman, she didn't want his attention at all!

She got up from the table, managing not to wince as her hip complained. "I'm going to look up some old friends."

"I think you should jog a few miles first."

"What?"

"Just thought I'd try it," he said wickedly, "since you usually take my suggestions and do the exact opposite. Cade, I need you. I need you to be one hundred per cent there tomorrow when you're observing me and that horse. I need you focused on us. You won't be able to do that if you overdo it today."

She sniffed. He was absolutely correct, of course, and she decided she might go and lie down for a while, though she wasn't going to let him see that. Imagine him talking to her as if she were some cranky old maid aunt who didn't have a penchant for doing what she was told!

She marched away, with her nose in the air. But not before she heard Dace's heartfelt sigh of long suffering.

Dace brought a portable stereo into the stall, hoping to calm Storm with some classical music. The horse hated confinement, and Dace hated seeing him burn his strength on jumpiness. He suspected that, until they figured out the horse, the other dreams would elude them. A gold medal was going to require every ounce of strength and energy both of them had, and Storm wore himself out with his restless pawing and fretting.

"I see he's still nervous inside."

Dace turned and saw the cold-eyed blond man. He recognized him. "Yeah," he said, his tone noncommittal.

"You've got a way with him."

Dace said nothing.

"You've got a way, period."

"What do you want?" Dace asked sharply.

"I'd like you to change stables. You're raw, but you seem to have some talent."

"I'm happy where I am," Dace said, aware of cold fury beginning to boil in his veins.

"Happiness is a pretty relative matter, isn't it? What's she paying you?"

"I said no."

"I've got a horse with every bit the potential of Storm——"

"Haven't you hurt her enough?" Dace cut him off with dangerous quiet.

Surprise registered in Lionel's face, and his eyes narrowed speculatively. "So it's not the money and not the horse. It must be the woman."

"Maybe you should look at the possibility it's *you* I wouldn't care to work for."

"Me? You don't even know me."

Dace walked slowly over to the door. He resisted an impulse to reach casually through the open top part of the box stall, twist his hands in Lionel's lapels and lift him off the ground. He eyed him evenly, and Lionel must have seen something in his eyes, because he backed off a step.

"I know you," Dace said softly. "Just who the hell do you think you are?"

"There's no need to get touchy. I was only speaking professionally. I used to coach her——"

"I said, I know who you are," Dace said quietly. It took every ounce of restraint he had not to smash his fist into that face. This was, after all, the creep who'd left her high and dry when she was hurt. The son of a dog who'd let her think she was nothing because she walked with a limp, because she couldn't ride any more. The son of a dog who'd temporarily declawed the tigress, taken her confidence in her own beauty and womanliness from her.

Dace turned abruptly away from him. Temporarily, Cadence had been shaken by her accident. A man like this one could never have hurt her permanently. It was probably because he knew it that he'd tried so hard, and kept on trying. He'd known long before the accident that he couldn't keep her. The accident had only made his knowledge worse.

"She's too much of a woman for you," Dace said softly. "You knew she'd grow up and leave you behind. The accident just made it easy for you to make it seem as if the flaw was hers instead of yours. What rot—as if a physical flaw can be compared to the handicap of a man who is so weak he's threatened by a good, strong woman."

"I could have Cadence back if I whistled."

Dace whirled toward the man. That was it! That was absolutely the limit!

Lionel was already walking away. "That horse will probably kill you. He's crazy," he called over his shoulder.

"Sure," Dace said dryly. "Why do I have the feeling you'd be the first one trying to buy him if he went up for sale?"

Dace felt far more aggravated than he wanted to feel. Did Cadence still have a soft spot for *that*? He had a baffled sense of wanting to throttle her over the very possibility, never mind the reality.

He frowned suddenly. He wondered why he cared. Oh, hell, the truth was probably that he'd cared from the first moment he saw her. It was something in him—to care for wounded things. She'd been a mystery he felt compelled to solve.

And now that he was coming closer to the solution? He laughed. Now he was being the fool. You didn't "solve" a woman like Cadence Copperthorne. Not unless you had a lifetime to do it in. And he wasn't doing that again. Not ever. Till death us do part was too painful a reality. He did not want to be responsible for another person's happiness ever again. One failure of that proportion was probably enough for any man to have on his conscience for a lifetime.

So what did he want? Why was he here? Why had he reacted so strongly to that man?

"To ride a Storm," he said, patting the big gray affectionately. "That's all, right, buddy?"

Storm's soft whinny sounded oddly mocking.

And yet he somehow knew he could no longer convince himself he was doing this for Sloan. When, somewhere in the back of his mind, a man started to formulate plans one step short of kidnap to prevent a woman's making a fool of herself over another man, then there were things stirring deep and hard within him.

The arrival of another visitor mercifully saved him from having to ponder that one for too long. Dace looked up to see himself being watched thoughtfully by a friendly looking, gray-haired man.

"Hi. Can I help you?"

"I recognized Storm. He's as magnificent as ever, isn't he?" A hand was extended over the gate. "I'm Dr. Masterson. I thought if I could find Storm, Cadence would be near by. Is she?"

"I can certainly understand your looking for her in proximity to storms," Dace said wryly, "but no, I don't know where she is."

"Too bad; I hoped to bump into her. She won't take my calls, and unfortunately I'm on my way home now."

Dace's eyes narrowed. "Can I give her a message?"

"Would you? Just tell her it's extremely important that she keep her appointments with me. And her physiotherapist. I've still got her scheduled at the regular times, and I won't fill that slot until I've heard from her."

For the second time in a very short period, Dace thanked his lucky stars that her slender neck wasn't anywhere in the vicinity of his hands.

Cadence felt a baffling anger in Dace for the rest of the day. She searched her mind for what she might have done wrong. After his openness and enthusiasm this morning this seemed like a dreadful slap in the face.

What was happening to her, where this man was concerned? She was relying rather heavily on what he thought of her, felt about her. Damn this passionate sport, and what it did to her emotions. It probably had nothing to do with that cowboy. It was the excitement of being back on her turf, feeling so at home, feeling as if she was where she belonged.

Cadence, a little voice inside her head chided, you revised your definition of passion the first time Dace laid his lips to you. She sighed. It was true. She'd thought her sport was what passion was all about, and then a few seconds of real passion, and her dream of gold had seemed like an oddly faded and colorless thing to spend one's life in pursuit of.

"Dace, did I do something wrong?" she asked, using an impatient tone to mask her uneasy mulling.

He looked at her, seemed to debate, and then gave her a slight smile. "Cadence, you only did something wrong if it's a crime to be born beautiful."

And then he grabbed her shoulders, placed a furious kiss on her astounded lips, backed away from her, shook his head, and turned his attention back to the stubborn horse.

"What was that all about?" she demanded.

"It was a peaceful substitute for what I really wanted to do," he muttered.

She stood there in stunned silence. After a long time she touched her lips tentatively with her index finger.

That confirmed it. It wasn't a passion for horses or for her sport that had been stirring in her veins all day, or, if it had been, that wasn't the kind of passion she was feeling now, because she gladly would have shot her horse to get Dace's undivided attention. Which he had decided not to give her.

She finally tossed her head and walked away.

Dace was aware the moment she left, and now he gave her his undivided attention, as he had refused to do while she stood there waiting for it.

He felt the breath go out of him at the sheer beauty of her. He realized that, until he'd had his talk with the doctor, her cane and her limp had failed to exist in his mind—except when she was so obviously in pain. He felt very irritated that her pain was self-induced—the by-product of her own neglect. But, if he was learning one thing about Cadence Copperthorne, it was that you didn't have much chance of winning an argument with her.

He was going to have to set out a big pot of honey to get Cadence Copperthorne to do something she wasn't eager to do. He was probably a fool to take it on. But then he never seemed to be able to back away from the pure challenge of her.

CHAPTER EIGHT

CADENCE was awakened by a sharp rapping on her door. She groaned and rolled over to look at the clock on her night table. Seven o'clock.

"Whadyawant?" she managed to mumble.

"It's Timothy, miss. Er—you have a guest."

She didn't answer. She snuggled down under her quilt. It was a dream, of course; people did not come calling at this hour.

"I'll handle it," she heard a deep familiar voice say.

Her eyes shot open.

"But, sir——"

"I'll be held accountable. Go back to bed."

"Er—well, very good."

If she weren't so startled she probably would have laughed. Timothy was completely unflappable. She had never seen him even slightly ruffled by any situation. But she could tell by his tone he was slightly ruffled now, and genuinely pleased, too.

Dace entered her room without knocking. He crossed his arms over his chest and stood there looking at her, a small smile playing across his lips.

"Good morning, Princess."

She was completely lost for words. She hadn't seen Dace dressed like this for a long time. He was wearing jeans faded nearly white, and a navy blue corduroy shirt. He had on a belt of tooled leather with a silver buckle, and a white cowboy hat with the same tooled leather on the brim. He looked gloriously masculine and for a moment she felt regret that she had taken him out of his natural habitat. Then she found her voice.

"Exactly what do you think you are doing?" she asked, her tone deliberately querulous. She pulled her quilt up to her nose.

He took off his hat, crossed the room, tossed the hat on her bed and then sat himself down on the edge of it. She scooted as far away from him as she could without falling out of bed. She eyed him warily—her heart was drumming so loudly in her ears that she thought she wouldn't be able to hear him when he spoke anyway. There was something absolutely sinful about a big, rugged man in his hardy work clothes looking so at home on priceless Chinese silk.

"How would you feel about an outing?"

"An outing?" she squeaked.

His eyes were intent on her face. "That's a nice old-fashioned word, isn't it? I like it." He leaned closer to her and lowered his voice to a whisper. "I especially like it when I don't plan to do anything as old-fashioned as bring a chaperon along."

"For heaven's sake, get off my bed! For heaven's sake, you big, cocksure oaf, what makes you think *I'll* be coming along?"

He made no move to get off her bed. He grinned at her tone, and she sank deeper underneath the quilt. Darn it, he seemed to be on to her—he wasn't going to be chased away by a hard, cool tone.

"Are you going to get dressed, or would you like some help?" he asked quietly.

Her mouth dropped open. "If you don't get out of here, I'll have Timothy throw you out."

Dace studied a fingernail thoughtfully. "Sent the poor old guy back to bed. Besides..." he shot her a fiendish grin "...he likes me."

"You mean he's been fooled by your silly cowboy charm. Well, that makes one."

"I think he has a romantic heart," Dace said thoughtfully.

"*Timothy?*"

"He seemed to be quite taken with the idea of a man coming calling with a horse and buggy. Of course, it does show more than your usual amount of flair and imagination——"

"A horse and buggy?" she whispered, her peevish facade falling away.

"And a picnic for two. Of course, if you don't want to come..." He got off the bed with a heartfelt sigh.

"I guess I could come," she said, regaining some composure and managing to make her tone quite careless.

That wicked grin spread. "I wasn't really going to take no for an answer."

"I don't see how you could have made me——" She stopped at the look on his face. If Dace said he wasn't taking no for an answer, he wasn't, and there was no sense challenging the man. Besides, she wanted to go with him.

"If you'll excuse me, I'll get dressed," she said, her nose tilted proudly.

"If you're sure you don't need any help——"

"Out!" she said, pointing imperiously to the door.

"Dress warm. There's a chill in the air this morning."

"Yes, sir."

"I've waited a long time for you to treat me with the respect I'm due," he teased.

"Out!" she commanded again.

He looked woeful. "Didn't think it would last." He picked up his cowboy hat and strolled out of her bedroom door.

She debated for a ridiculous length of time about what to wear. Finally she wore a yellow plaid skirt with a touch of lace peeping out below the hem, low-heeled Western boots, and a lace-edged blouse under a yellow sweater. She fastened her hair back loosely with a matching yellow ribbon and eyed herself critically in the mirror.

She looked nice, she decided, almost shyly. High color burned in her cheeks and a hopeful light shone in her eyes. She looked just right for a ride in a horse and buggy, with just a hint of the old-fashioned in the way she was dressed. For once, she didn't even change her opinion of how she looked when she added the cane.

Dace was outside the front door, his face tilted to the warming rays of the morning sun. He turned at the click of the front door, and looked at her. She didn't feel awkward as she moved across the veranda to him. Something told her that Dace didn't even see the limp; that he only saw what was loveliest about her. His eyes trailed, with muted appreciation, over every detail of her appearance, and she was delighted that she had been so painstaking.

"You look beautiful," he murmured huskily, when she stopped in front of him. "I've never seen you wear a skirt before. It suits you."

For so long now she hadn't worn dresses because she thought they accentuated her limp—made it more apparent, made a mockery of her attempts to be feminine.

She was a captive of his eyes for a long time, before she forced herself to look away from him. The morning was crisp, frost still clinging to the ground.

"Oh, for heaven's sake," she breathed. Parked at the bottom of the step was an old-fashioned, two-seater covered buggy. "Where did you find that contraption?"

"Sloan collects them and restores them to working order."

"And he lent it to *you*?"

"I happen to be a very responsible human being——"

"You happen to be a renegade," she murmured.

"——besides which, Sloan knows even I wouldn't try and jump a horse that had a buggy attached to it."

He helped her up on to the deep leather bench then went around and climbed up beside her. He took the reins in his hand and clicked to the horse who moved off at a nice steady walk. He clicked again and they moved to a trot. They came to the Copperthorne gate and turned on to the main road.

"What a lovely way to travel," she murmured. The morning was beautiful—made even more intensely so by the steady clip-clopping of the horse's hoofs, the lovely, lulling rock of the buggy... and by the presence of the man who sat beside her.

Now and then a car would go by, and the occupants would smile knowingly and wave. Cadence felt ridiculously happy—like a little girl in a parade. She always waved back.

After a while they turned off the main road. Dace got down and opened a gate, so they could follow a track down to a grove of cottonwoods and the creek which she could see in the distance.

"Is this Copperthorne land?" she asked curiously. She didn't think it was, but you could never tell what her father had been up to.

"No. This is Stanton land."

She looked down the road. It seemed to wind on forever without a fence. "All of it?" she asked.

"Yeah, I guess there's a fair bit of it."

She turned and looked at him narrowly. "I didn't know you had land. Why didn't you tell me?"

"What for, Cade? I figured sooner or later you'd get my measure as a man. I don't think what I own, or don't own, has much to do with that, personally."

"You let me believe you were an ambitionless cowboy."

"How long did you believe that for?"

She got his point. "About thirty seconds," she murmured with a smile and a shake of her head.

He stopped the horse and buggy, and passed her the reins. "Okay—your turn."

She stared down at the reins. The leather felt good in her hands. How she had missed that feeling. She hesitated, and then clicked her tongue and slapped the reins. The horse moved amiably ahead.

"Let's speed it up," Dace suggested.

She moved the horse into a trot.

"Let's go, Cadence."

She flashed him a look, and then slapped the reins again. The horse broke into a smooth canter. The wind caught in her face and the thunder of hoofs rang in her ears. The carriage jolted over a bump

in the road and she almost lost her seat. She burst
out laughing. She laughed into the wind, she
laughed until the tears rolled down her face. Finally,
as they started to go down a hill toward the distant
creek, she reined the horse in, allowing herself again
to appreciate the feeling of deep pleasure that
having leather between her fingers gave her.

She passed the reins back to him. "Thanks, Dace.
It wasn't the same, but thanks."

"I never intended for it to be the same," he said
slowly. "But before you had nothing. Now you have
something. That's all. Sloan said to tell you the
buggy's yours. Any time you want it, he'll get it
ready for you."

She could feel a lump growing in her throat. No,
it wasn't the same. But still, when she wanted to
be out in the fresh morning, in the early evening,
when she wanted to be out and *part* of the landscape, she could. She could still have part of it. Not
the exciting part; but the slow, languid, lovely part
of being around horses. The part that transported
her back into a different time and age, she could
have. And that was a very special gift.

"Don't go crying on me, Cadence Copperthorne," he said softly.

"Ha!" she said, swiping a tear from her cheek.
"You should know better by now!"

He was smiling knowingly at her. "I do know
better."

They had stopped in a grove of cottonwoods. It
had taken them quite a while to get here and the
dew was gone from the ground. He helped her
down, then pulled a huge wicker basket out of the
back of the buggy. He spread a blanket in the tall
grass.

"Is this *still* your land?" she asked, once she was seated.

"Mmm. You want some champagne?"

She laughed. "For breakfast? That sounds frightfully decadent. And delicious."

"It's mixed with orange juice," he said. She watched as he poured hers into a long-stemmed plastic wineglass, but then he poured himself hot coffee from a Thermos.

"Oh-oh," she mused. "Are you planning on getting me drunk and seducing me?"

He laughed, a pleasant rumble that came deep from his belly. "I may be planning one, but not the other," he teased. He cocked an eyebrow at her. "Care to guess which one?"

"You're making me nervous," she said, and he was. "Don't you drink?"

He hesitated for a long time, and then drew in a deep breath. "No. Not any more."

There was a note of unbelievable pain in his voice, and she waited for him to go on. In a while, he did.

"My wife, Janey, and my little girl, Jasmine, were killed in a fire four and a half years ago. Jasmine was only five."

She remembered that night she and Dace had shared a starry sky, and she remembered guessing he carried some terrible tragedy within him. But she had compared it to her own tragedy, and her own was so puny in comparison to this.

"Dace, I'm so sorry." The words seemed so small.

"There's sorrow," he confided quietly, "and lots of it, though the years seem to take the edge off the sorrow. But there was some guilt involved, too, and that cut is still the deepest.

"When I took over the family ranch it just seemed as if there was so much pressure all the time. I was a boy, dealing with a man's pressures. Janey was a neighbor girl, and she was always there, doing her best to make me feel like a grown-up. We got married, because we had to, when we were both nineteen. I'm ashamed to say I even felt quite manly about that.

"But I never loved her. Janey wasn't strong— you couldn't look at her sideways without her crying. I was always trying to pretend I was happy so she'd quit trying so hard, but pretending is hard work, and it killed us in its own way. I started leaving her on her own a lot. I felt as if I were always walking on eggshells around her. A man needs to get decently angry every now and then, he needs to be able to be grouchy as a bear in his own house if he wants to. But I felt Janey was too fragile to handle the real me, and I felt lonely and annoyed and impatient around her. I threw myself into the ranch work. Those are hard memories to live with. That I didn't give my wife or my daughter the time they deserved."

"Not very many teen marriages are made in heaven, Dace."

"I know."

"You needed a strong, strong woman."

She felt his eyes move to her face and fasten there. "I know," he said again, his voice a whisper softer than the breeze that caressed her cheek.

"After my wife and daughter died, I hit the bottle pretty hard. Sloan rescued me somewhere before I succeeded in killing myself, but not before I'd lost a whole herd of pure-blooded Charolais cattle."

"Sloan rescued you?"

"He and my dad were good friends. They both grew up right around here; cowboyed together for a long time. He kind of kept an eye on me after my dad died, and gave me advice I never took. When I started getting into Charolais he didn't approve—said my family was paying the price for my ambition. And it was true, but I didn't want to hear that. And after the fire it made me resent him that he knew I'd been so busy and wrapped up with my blooded stock cattle that I barely knew my wife or my little girl. He came around but I wouldn't have anything to do with him. Usually wouldn't even invite him in.

"Meanwhile I was selling off my cattle to support my excesses, and in some perverse way trying to come out even. If I got rid of the cattle that made everybody but me so unhappy...

"Anyway, one day Sloan showed up, took one look at me, and knocked me cold. He packs quite a punch for an old guy," Dace said ruefully. "I woke up in his house, being spoon-fed soup and told he needed a hand for branding, if I thought I could stay sober that long.

"He threw me a lifeline, and somehow, probably with a lot of grace, I managed to grab it. I've been at the ranch ever since. And I know the truth: I'd be dead by now, if Sloan hadn't shown up that day. I owe him my life—and he knows it. And, to answer your original question, no, I don't drink any more. Scares the hell out of me where that almost got me."

"You're lucky you didn't lose the land," she commented.

He looked over it, and she could see his love for it in his eyes. "Some day, I'd like to rebuild a herd and ranch it again. It's been in the family for generations. I grew up on this land. My daddy ranched it all his life."

"You grew up on this land? We grew up within a few miles of each other?"

"We wouldn't have hung out in the same circles, Cadence Copperthorne," he said wryly.

"I did go to private school—and, of course, you're years older than me," she teased.

"Cadence, sometimes you just don't use your head. Here you sit, in the middle of nowhere, entirely at my mercy for a ride home, and you start throwing insults around."

"Not smart," she agreed with a laugh. "What do I have to do to wriggle back into your good graces?"

"Tell me about you."

She looked into his eyes—he really wanted to know. She glanced away into the distance. "There's embarrassingly little to tell. My whole life has been spent trying to make my dream of a gold medal a reality. I never even had a boyfriend, because they always got in the way of my training, of the time I wanted to spend with my horses.

"It's the only dream I ever had. This might sound like poor little rich girl, but kids need something to aspire to. My dad was too softhearted to understand that. Anything I asked for he just gave me. I think he was trying to make up for the fact that I didn't have a mom. She died when I was three. I hear she was a lot like me—especially in temperament. I needed something to work toward— I was a wild, spirited kid. I needed to achieve something for myself—not have it given to me.

"When I was twelve——" she smiled at her brashness "—I won my first equestrian event. A few months earlier, my dad had taken me to see the Olympic equestrian events. I decided that was what I wanted, and I set out to get it.

"Somewhere along the way I got engaged to a man who didn't love me, and who ditched me after the accident. So, until you came along, I was the proud owner of some shattered dreams. Now, I hope maybe I can rescue some remnants of them."

"Did you love him? The man you were engaged to?" His voice was gravelly.

"I guess, in a way, I did. I certainly believed I did at the time."

"I saw you kiss him once. A kiss like that could meld the shattered glass of a few dreams back together."

She ducked her head and felt a fiery glow moving up her face.

His voice was rough. "Cadence, I need to know. I need to know how things stand between you and him."

She didn't want to give him that. She had used Lionel like a shield ever since she'd met Dace, and now he was asking her to throw it away. She wasn't sure she was ready.

"So. That's how it is," he said softly, misreading her hesitation.

She looked at him defiantly. "I only kissed Lionel that day to give a certain arrogant cowboy a 'hands off' message. It didn't work worth a hill of beans."

"I'm asking you if you still have a soft spot for him," Dace persisted grimly. "I'm asking you if you still lie awake at night and think of him, of the way it felt when he held you and touched you, and kissed you."

She decided not to admit to Dace that the thought of Lionel's kisses had never kept her awake at night. She decided not to admit anything.

"I'm asking if you'd go back to him if you had the chance." There was a note of something close to pain in that deep voice, and she looked at him in surprise.

"What's it to you, Dace?"

"Don't ask to see my cards without showing me yours."

She sighed. "Lionel and I, we shared a dream once, and when the dream was gone we didn't have anything left. Nothing."

Dace nodded thoughtfully. Something in his face relaxed. "I don't think it's whether we attain our dreams that gives us our mark as people, Cadence. I think it's how we handle their breaking like glass in front of us that is the real tribute to our human spirit. He wasn't strong enough for you."

"I know," she whispered. "I need a strong man." Flustered by her admission, she stammered, "To win that gold medal for me, of course."

"Cadence, it's a long shot. At best, it's a long shot. You don't need a gold medal to make you something. You don't have to earn your right to breathe air. You are and that's enough. You have to make that enough. You have to start putting that before the dream."

"What do you mean?" she asked, startled by the sudden sternness of his expression.

"I bumped into Dr. Masterson at the show."

"Damn," she said.

"I assumed from the message he asked me to pass along to you that you hadn't been keeping your appointments with him. Or the physiotherapist."

"Thank you for that message. Isn't that a lovely bird over there? What do you suppose it's called?"

"A robin," Dace said dryly.

"Yes, I've always liked robins," she mused thoughtfully. "I've always——"

"Cadence, be quiet. Don't try and change the subject. It won't work. You are guilty of neglecting yourself, and I want your promise that those appointments will be kept."

"It's no concern of yours, Dace Stanton," she said, just a trace of shrillness entering her voice. She suspected this little talking-to was the real object of this seemingly romantic outing, and it hurt dreadfully. As he had pointed out earlier, she was at his mercy, virtually his prisoner.

She felt furious. Outmaneuvered. She'd laid all her cards on the table, and he was still holding his close to his chest. Not only that, he was now going after something completely different.

"You're going to start going again next week, or else——"

"Or else what?" she taunted him, her cheeks blazing.

"Or else, I'm going to quit riding for you."

"How dare you threaten me with that?"

"No, Cadence. How dare you put something like that ahead of your responsibility to yourself? I'll work for you, and I'll work hard for you, but only as long as I know you're working equally hard on yourself."

She stood up and brushed some crumbs off her skirt. "Take me home."

He folded his arms across his chest. "No."

"You have some nerve," she said quietly, looking down into his face. "Do you remember that day I got you into the riding shop and you called me sneaky and manipulative? That was the Flying Nun compared to this——"

He shrugged. "Remember I pointed something out to you once? The same ingredients only mixed up differently? Besides, I don't understand your objection to looking after yourself; to regaining as much of your mobility as you can."

"So I can be her again? The one you spy on in your room at night?"

"You make it sound as if you're the star of a girlie magazine instead of a video most people would find incredibly boring."

"What is your interest in getting me back to the doctor?"

"For pity's sake, Cadence, you're in pain about ninety per cent of the time!"

"I still don't see——"

He knocked her legs out from under her and she collapsed back onto the blanket. She sputtered indignantly and tried to rise, but he was on top of her, his eyes unbearably close, hissing smoky blue sparks.

"I care about you. Is that so bloody hard for you to believe?"

A shock trembled through her. Were these his cards? No, he didn't mean that the way she wanted him to mean it.

"As a matter of fact, yes. As a matter of fact——"

His voice was an angry rasp. "You know, in all the time I've known you, I've only figured out one way to shut you up."

"I don't want to shut up," she informed him. "You can't make me——"

His lips stole her breath away.

He was angry, and the anger came through his lips, and through the hard tension in his body where it pinned hers to the blanket. He was so hard, so strong, so crushing.

Helplessly she wrapped her arms around him to pull his hardness and his strength yet closer. The texture of the kiss changed at that. His lips trailed over hers. He conquered her mouth, plundered it gently. His hands moved to her hair, and he stripped the yellow ribbon from it, and ran his hands through the wild tangle of it.

"You are so beautiful," he murmured.

She felt a pleased jolt at that. He meant it. He meant it to the bottom of his socks.

She took his head between her hands, and met his mouth with her own. With gentle aggression she told him how much he meant to her. She did need him. And it didn't have a thing to do with some faraway gold medal.

The need was a burning thing inside her, something she had never felt before. Her world had been too consumed with horses, and high dreams. Her energies had been poured out into the pursuit of her ideals. She had never had anything left—had never even realized what she was missing.

The woman in her had had no opportunity to come out. There had been no passion or energy left over for that.

And yet now that it had this was the only part of her that mattered. That had ever mattered. Oh, if that accident had some higher purpose, perhaps it was this. That she discover what it was to be a woman. That it was a necessary part of herself to be a woman. That it was a part of herself that was not to be denied.

His hands were under her sweater. Bold. Tender. Exploring. He found the clasp to her bra and unhitched it with expert hands.

"I've been dreaming of doing that for weeks," he informed her, his voice a sensuous growl, "ever since this thing made an appearance."

"It's your own fault."

"I know," he told her huskily, in between nibbles on her ear and neck. "You can't begin to imagine how a man wishes he could take back words spoken with such a complete lack of foresight."

The wisp of lace and silk appeared from under her sweater and he tossed it carelessly away.

His hand sought the unveiled sculpture of her breast, and she gasped with unbearable passion and pleasure when his fingers spread over the mound, teased her nipple slowly and languorously as a summer breeze stirring the branches of a tree.

"How do you make love?" he whispered, nibbling at her ear.

She felt herself stiffen with embarrassment and tension. "What?"

"You said you couldn't do it normally. I've been wondering ever since..."

"I don't know," she croaked, mortified.

He laughed into her throat. "I was hoping you would say that."

"What? Dace, what?"

"I was hoping that you and I were going to unlock the secrets of pleasuring you together."

His eyes met hers, and she stared into them, astounded by what she saw there.

"I'm scared," she whispered.

"Me, too, Princess," he murmured into her ear. "Me, too."

CHAPTER NINE

SOMEHOW they'd ended up underneath the blanket, tangled together. Now that other sensations were receding, the bed of lush, sweet grass tickled Cade's back, her skin more receptive to sensation than it had ever been. She looked up at the sky, and it seemed its beauty would overwhelm her, swallow her.

Dace was lying on his stomach. His arm, strong and brown, was thrown across her midriff. The weight was comforting. His nose was touching her jawbone, and his breath tickled the nape of her neck.

"Are you crying?" he asked, his voice deep and low and gentle as his loving had been.

"Yes."

"Did I hurt you, after all?" He sat up on one elbow and looked down into her face with concern.

"No, Dace, you didn't hurt me."

"Why didn't you tell me?" he demanded softly.

"Tell you? Oh, that..." She smiled. "Would you have done something differently?"

He ran a hand through the shining curls of his hair. "I guess I would have."

"That's why I didn't tell you."

"Please stop crying."

"A woman cries for a lot of reasons. Right now I just feel happy. And whole and alive in a way I never felt before."

"I didn't plan this," he said gruffly.

"Didn't you?" She didn't know whether to feel dismayed or amused. She didn't seem to have much choice what to feel anyway—the heavy, relaxed languor had totally invaded her body, mind and soul.

"I lost my head."

"Hmm."

"Cadence, you're not the kind of woman a man takes lightly."

"Is the double meaning intended?" she teased from her safe, warm cloud of contentment.

"Cade, you know what I mean."

"No, I don't," she said honestly.

"You're not the kind of woman who takes a man lightly."

"Double meaning——"

"Cadence! Things are never going to be the same between us."

"Is that bad?"

"Lord, I don't know."

"Does it feel bad right now?"

"You know it doesn't. You know it feels like a little piece of heaven right now."

"Can't it feel like this all the time?" she said, tracing her finger over the hard plane of his shoulder, down the corded muscles of his arm. The pure physical strength of him caused her awe—the way he had tempered all that power made her begin to tingle all over again.

"Yes," he said huskily, leaning toward her. "No!" He leapt back. "Cade, right now it's hard to think. About the other things."

"What other things?"

"Have you ever washed a dish, Cadence? Cooked a meal? Swept a floor?"

"I thought feminism had put an end to discussions like this," she mused, oddly unthreatened by his doubts.

"Feminism? *I* wash dishes, and cook, and sweep floors. I don't have maids and butlers and——"

"Oh, I get it."

"Do you?" His tone softened. "Have you ever looked at a dress or a diamond or a car and not been able to have it?"

"I don't see what that has to do with what just happened."

"No? It's about the difference in our realities."

"Oh, Dace! We made love. Isn't this the modern new world where people do things like that without pledging their lives to each other?"

"Thoroughly modern Cadence," he snorted. "I might even believe you if your old-fashioned virginity hadn't been intact."

"You're the one who's trying to make it into something more!"

"Your eyes are telling me something I'm not ready to hear," he proclaimed softly. "You're not the kind of woman I could have an affair with. And you're not the kind of woman I could marry either."

"Why?"

"I can't have an affair with you because it wouldn't be enough. And I can't marry you because I can't afford you. Besides, I've seen firsthand what marriage does to two fairly nice people."

"That's a dilemma, all right," she said coldly, fury and hurt sweeping away the cloud of her contentment like an icy wind.

"Oh, hell, Cadence." He reached for her. "I can't keep my hands off you, either."

"I guess I could probably learn to sweep a floor," she murmured, her anger dying and being replaced by this odd, unfurling flag of hope.

"I can't ask you that."

"Of course, you'd have to sweep them, too."

"You're too bossy by far, Cadence."

"Mmm." She let her hand drift under the blanket.

"And far too beautiful."

"I don't really even like diamonds."

"Dammit. You're a witch. I knew right from the beginning that you were a witch. What am I going to do with you?"

"Love me?" she suggested.

"Yeah," he growled. "There's always that."

"Dace, I'm not interested in tomorrow. Or your promises. I just want right now."

"I don't believe you, Cade. A woman like you isn't going to take any less than a man's soul."

She silenced him with her lips. Later, she assured herself, much later, she would look at the consequences of loving a man who could talk about affairs and marriage without ever mentioning the word love.

She wished she didn't love him. It would hurt so much less if she didn't love him. But she knew with an aching, hurting tenderness that she did. She loved him. And she had loved him for a long time.

"I'm supposed to ride tomorrow, you know," he managed to tell her in between kisses. "At Cedar Park."

"I think we might be finished by tomorrow," she assured him, turning her head to nibble on the curve of his chin.

"I just wondered if you were one of those coaches."

"What coaches?"

"The kind who thinks making love saps an athlete's energy. Who orders celibacy——"

"No," she said firmly, "I'm definitely not that kind of coach."

"Hmm. You must be the other kind, then."

"The other kind?"

"The kind who encourages athletes to——"

"Yes," she whispered eagerly. "I'm that kind."

"Good," he said throatily. "Because I'm that kind of athlete."

"Of course, you could always quit riding if this proved detrimental."

He laughed. "I want *that* in writing."

"I thought you dealt on handshakes?" she teased him.

"Not if I can get something better."

"You snake——"

"Only with you," he assured her, then pulled her on top of him and stared into her eyes. "If you're feeling any pain, you have to tell me, okay? Don't be brave about it. Or shy. I don't want to hurt you."

"It doesn't hurt," she whispered. Except her heart had a funny little hurt in it—a kind of overwhelming tenderness for the man who lay with her among the crushed grass and wildflowers. It made her feel very vulnerable to care about anybody as much as she cared about Dace Stanton.

But, in truth, it wasn't because they had become lovers that she was feeling this way. This was a culmination of things that she had been feeling since she had first laid eyes on this lean, handsome cowboy.

She smiled. She knew she really had believed he could ride Storm, but now she also wondered if her heart hadn't used his skill in the saddle as a way to outmaneuver her defences. Thank goodness for hearts that wouldn't die, for spirits that still danced even after they'd been wounded.

As for his not knowing where they were going or what he wanted, well, so what? She knew life didn't have any guarantees anyway. She knew that you could plan and plot and schedule and scheme and come no closer to ever getting what you wanted.

Sometimes life had a few unexpected twists and turns, and it was in those unexpected, unplanned places where all the treasure was hidden. If you could outrun the booby traps.

"In that case, if you want a really good ride tomorrow, I suggest you kiss me."

She kissed him.

When she watched him the next day, at the horse show, she was very much aware that he looked different to her. That she was seeing him with brand-new eyes—not as a man, but as *her* man. Brand-new eyes as she participated in this age-old rite of passage—a woman looking at the man who had become her lover. She marveled at the wind playing with his hair, and the ripple of bronzed muscles beneath his clothing. Her eyes strayed to his lips and his hands and his eyes, tickling the memories within her. She felt the secret and thrilling pleasure of knowing things of him that no one else here could know. Intimate secrets. How smooth and unblemished was the skin over corded muscle. How clear and seeking his eyes were after he made love. How tender those large, strong hands could be.

He sat the horse like a warrior of old, something fearlessly calm in him that embraced the elements of danger, and eagerly anticipated the challenge.

Yes, she had always looked at him with a kind of pure feminine appreciation. But now she looked at him differently again. The world was a little brighter around the edges because he was in it. He seemed electrically alive, and everything else seemed faded and dull. Now, she saw him with a lover's possessiveness and it did extraordinary things to her heart to see this self-possessed, magnificently attractive man, and think, He's mine. And tonight, when all of this is over, he'll cradle me in those same arms that are so effortlessly holding that horse in check, he'll capture me with those same steel-strong legs that he uses to guide the horse, he'll unleash on me the power that he keeps such a tight leash on when he rides Storm.

She could feel a flush starting up her cheeks. He was hers. For now. But he'd already warned her he wouldn't or couldn't stay. She didn't know what to do about that. Her pride told her to call it quits before he did. Her ego told her to get out now before she got in too deeply, and the hurt of getting back out became unbearable.

And her heart told her to ride the storm for as long as it lasted. Her heart told her to accept the unexpected gifts of life exactly as they were given. Without expectation or regret. Without looking backward or forward.

Dace, who had been focusing on the course, riding the jumps and planning his strategy in his mind, turned, as suddenly as if she had called him,

and looked at her. And she knew, from the unguarded tenderness that flashed through his eyes,
that for now, for this moment in time, her heart
was safe in this man's keeping.

His name and number were called, and he
snapped the chin strap closed, touched the brim of
his cap to her, and then, with utter and compelling
confidence, guided Storm into the ring.

With effort Cadence forced herself to focus on
the task at hand. Storm was going beautifully today.
He was calm and good-mannered, responsive and
obedient. He always jumped superbly when he was
like this; as effortlessly as though he were part eagle.

A warning whistle blew and Dace nudged the big
gray into that easy, powerful lope. They completed
one tight circle and then approached the first jump.

It was a harder course than anything they had
practiced, Cadence observed. But if they were
nervous it didn't show. All that showed on Dace's
face was total concentration. He was so focused on
the course, and the horse, and the jumps, that the
rest of the world must have disappeared for him.
It was a feeling she remembered well.

Her own nervousness disappeared and was replaced with a slow awe. They were beautiful. They
were everything that this sport was about—
boldness, and heart, and incredible discipline. They
were poetry, absolute and effortless poetry, as they
sailed, a complete team, over one jump after
another.

She felt a single moment of jealousy for the world
she had left behind—for the feel of that magnificent horse surging underneath her, giving his whole
huge heart to the job in front of him. And then
even that was gone. She could still share it. Dace

knew how she felt, and he was so good at describing for her every sensation, every nuance of feeling, every reaction of the horse to his every command. He sensed her hunger for details and provided them with good humor and grace.

She could feel a certain sizzling tension building in the silence of the crowd and she looked around. She could see they were beginning to see what she had always seen. There wasn't so much as the rattle of a popcorn container coming from the crowded stands as every eye focused on the man and the horse. Rarely, ever so rarely, a man and a horse performed like this. With a unity of spirit that was awe inspiring, with a compatibility of grace and strength and power that were unbelievable.

She turned back to them; back to her dream of the gold. She knew it would come true. She simply knew, in that moment, that she had never lost the dream, that it had only been postponed.

She would remember that moment of certainty for the rest of her life, and wonder if it had incensed the gods that she still wanted. That, even though last night she had been given more than she had ever dared expect from her life, she still wanted more.

Out of nowhere, with absolutely no warning, Storm went berserk. He had been loping steadily toward his next jump, when suddenly he corkscrewed sideways and began to run.

Dace's expression hardly changed, except that a determined line whitened around his mouth. His horsemanship was superb. In fact, she could tell that he had ridden a bucking bronc or two, and that experience stood him in good stead now. But he was pitting his strength against the strength of a formidable opponent. The horse was in a complete panic. He didn't even seem to be slightly taken aback by Dace's attempts to get him under control.

Over the loudspeaker, far away, she could hear an announcer saying something about one of the finest demonstrations of horsemanship he had ever seen. And it was true— Dace was showing amazing skill. Obviously everything he'd ever learned about horses was being poured into this moment. When it became evident he could not halt the horse, he stopped trying, and resigned himself to guiding the movement as much as he could. He managed to maneuver Storm out of the hazardous area of the jumps and began to manipulate him into a large circle around the perimeter of the arena.

The horse was wild-eyed, beginning to froth under his saddle and at the mouth. Cadence wondered, sickly, if he could run forever. She was so proud of Dace for not bailing out, for sticking with it—for being able to stick with it.

And just when it looked as if Dace would win Storm abruptly changed direction, fighting the rein, and throwing Dace off balance. He charged the permanent boundary fence that surrounded the jump area. He hit it like a steamroller. The fence splintered. Dace went down, and Storm sprang free.

Dace lay in a crumpled heap, among the litter of the fence, blood seeping from underneath his helmet, down his face.

By the time she reached him a crowd had formed around him. He was beginning to stir, but he had lain deathly still for just long enough for her to imagine the abyss that life would become without him in it.

Suddenly, she felt foolishly and angrily naive that he had not made her the promise of forever that just moments ago she had been so blithely sure she could live without.

She sank down beside him and took his hand. She was reassured by the strength in it, the resiliency of his skin, the warmth. He opened his eyes, and stared at her. He tried to smile, and them grimaced from effort.

"Geez, Cade," he mumbled, "what did you hit me with?"

In a matter of minutes, he was stubbornly blocking the attempts of the first-aid people to get him on to a stretcher. He walked off the field, to thunderous applause.

"Where's Storm?" He tried, unsuccessfully, to shake off the grip of the muscular young man who was the first-aid attendant. "Would you let go of me?" he snapped.

"No, sir. You'd probably fall over if I did. That wound has to be bandaged. It looks as if you have some fragments of wood imbedded in your skull."

"Thick as it is," Cadence said, and was rewarded with a glare. She reached out and touched his face. Her hand came away smeared with blood, and she shoved it under his nose.

"Oh, hell," he said, as if bleeding to death were a nuisance he didn't have time for right now. But she knew he was weaker than he appeared when he allowed himself to be led over to the grassy area where the first-aid vehicle was parked.

Dace looked suspiciously at the ambulance. He refused to go in it. The ambulance attendant wisely saw the need for compromise, and opened the back doors so that Dace could sit in the doorway, with one of those long legs firmly planted on green grass.

"It looks worse than it is," the ambulance attendant assured Cadence, as he cleaned the wound. It was fairly obvious to him that his patient was not patient—and not the least bit interested in the proceedings. "Head wounds bleed a lot. But," he said to Dace, "it'll probably be a couple of days before you are doing much of anything. And there's a chance of concussion——"

Dace grunted impatiently. "Would you just hurry up?"

The young man seemed to become even more meticulous in his dressing of the wound—winding a white gauze around the now cleaned wound. Cadence silently thanked him.

"What's your hurry?" she asked Dace.

"I doubt if they've managed to catch Storm yet."

"I don't know if they've caught him," she said coldly, "and I don't care. My father was right about that horse. He should be shot."

Dace was frowning. "No. In that second when I felt him start to twist underneath me, something clicked. For a second I knew why he was doing it. But I can't remember right now."

"It doesn't matter. Not right now." Not ever again, she decided. She could not subject the man she loved to the danger of an unpredictable horse over and over again. Something was going to have to be done. Right now, she was angry enough to think the only solution was a shotgun. Which, considering her loyalty and affection to the horse, was a very strong statement about the power of her feelings for Dace.

"Now," said the young man, looking proudly at his bandaging job, "why don't you just come lie down in the back here until your head clears a bit?"

Dace stood up. He wavered.

"Dace," Cadence crooned, "just lie down for a——"

At precisely that moment Storm thundered by, frothing and frenzied, but not looking nearly as frenzied as the harried officials who were chasing him.

"For heaven's sake," Dace breathed. He swung in that direction and Cadence clutched his arm.

"They can manage without you, Dace."

"Did it look as if they were managing?" he asked, looking askance at the hand on his arm. "I'm going to find a rope. I think I can——"

She shuddered inwardly at the vision of him being dragged behind the horse that shot through her mind. He'd been through enough and so had she.

She didn't move her hand. Her lip trembled. "I need you right now. And I don't want to talk about that horse."

"Cade, you know Storm as well as I do. And chances are not a soul is going to be able to get near him. The highway is too close to the grounds. They'll kill him if it isn't handled right."

"Good."

He sighed impatiently. "You must be in shock. You won't feel that way in a while. Besides, something clicked——"

"So you said once before," she said coldly, knowing she was losing.

"I have to go. That's in my blood. You can't take the cowboy out of me, Cade, and a cowboy looks after his horse. First and last. That's all there is to it.''

"And what about the woman? Where do I fit into your stupid, corny cowboy code of honor?''

"Cadence, you're not in need. You're not scared and hurting. He could be hurt.''

"I *am* scared and hurting. I don't want you running around with a fractured skull after a mad horse.''

"I have a cut on my head. I don't have a fractured skull. And the horse isn't mad.'' He looked at her long and hard. "This isn't how it works, Cadence.''

"How what works?'' she demanded, but she didn't like the resignation in his tone—as if this was something he knew he would have to tell her.

"This isn't about Storm. It's about you and me. You don't own a person because you've made love to them. Not even if you love them. Love isn't about owning. It's not about always having your way. It's not about making me choose between you and what I feel my duty is.''

"I'm going to have the horse shot,'' she said, because she was so angry with him. She had been so careful not to mention the word love. She had been so careful not to do exactly what he was saying she was doing anyway. But she did love him and he was choosing a horse over her. Damned cowboy!

"All the more reason I'd better get to him,'' he said wryly. "Look, it probably won't take long. They may have him under control already...'' His tone was dubious. "Why don't you go get some supper, and I'll come find you as soon as I can, all right?''

"Don't bother!" she spat out viciously. "I'm going to leave now."

His eyes held hers sternly and then he shrugged. "Have it your way. I have better things to do than spend my time with a willful, spoiled brat."

She raised her hand, and he caught it in an iron grip.

"The next time you raise your hand to me, or throw your cane at me, I'm going to turn you over my knee and give you a damned good licking."

He let her go, turned and walked rapidly away. For a single moment she debated throwing her cane at him for the pure pleasure of diverting his aggravatingly one-track mind. For the pure pleasure of challenging him, calling his bluff.

He turned and gave her one last look, and she had the uneasy feeling he might have read her mind. She gave her head a spirited toss. No sense giving him the satisfaction of knowing that when he looked so grimly forbidding she had about as much nerve as a chastened child.

When Dace finally found Storm the scenario was very much as he'd imagined. A group of well-meaning officials had suspended a rope between themselves and had Storm trapped by some buildings. Dace bit back the temptation to tell them how to use a rope. At least the horse wasn't running up the highway.

It was obvious the horse was exhausted. Storm was trembling and bleeding badly from a gash in his chest.

"We just got him again," one of the men informed Dace. "The vet's going to tranquillize him

in a minute, if we can hang on to him. We've been
at this stage twice before.''

Dace approached Storm slowly, talking calmly
and gently. The horse's head drooped with relief at
the sound of the familiar voice. Dace walked up to
him and touched his shoulder. The horse responded by laying his head on Dace's hands.

Dace looked at the snapped reins. "You're lucky
you didn't break a leg," he remonstrated with mock
sternness.

It seemed like hours before he got the tired but
still stubborn horse looked at by a vet, and loaded
into the trailer. He caught a glimpse of himself in
a mirror and saw blood had seeped through the pure
white of the bandage. His clothes were torn and
dirty. He looked like a guerrilla commando. Which
was probably just about what one had to be to have
a relationship with Cadence Copperthorne.

On impulse, he dropped the horse off at a se-
cluded paddock on his land. No use trying to get
him into a stable tonight—and no use finding out
how powerful an anger Cadence would hold inside
her.

He realized he half hoped she would be over being
mad by the time he got home. He fantasized about
her to be waiting for him in his apartment, all soft
and sexy and needing to be kissed. But when he
drove in the lights were out over the stable. He
glanced hopefully across the yard toward her
bedroom window. Her window was uninvitingly
black.

He sighed. He was bone-weary anyway. And she
was a redhead; it would probably take her a few
days to cool out. Lord, she was sexy when she was

spitting yellow sparks out of those awesome amber
eyes.

He frowned, and took one last look "the castle."
She came from a different world from his, that was
for sure. He had his land, and he had money put
away, and some day he knew he'd be a prosperous
rancher again. But he knew he was never going to
be able to keep Cadence Copperthorne in the
manner to which she was accustomed. And he
didn't know what to do about that.

"Lady," he whispered into the night, "maybe
you're best to stay over there." The words caused
an unbelievable anguish to flash through him.

He entered his apartment, and even though he
was dead tired he went and put on the video. He
had looked at it close to a hundred times trying to
figure out what happened.

Tonight, it hit him like a ton of bricks.

Of course, he thought, of course! And now that
he knew what it was it amazed him that he had
never figured it out before. Now, it seemed so
glaringly obvious.

As obvious as it had been as soon as that horse
had corkscrewed out from underneath him this
afternoon. All those hours of sitting in front of this
video had clicked then. In that split second when
he had heard the siren and simultaneously felt the
horse twist under him.

And here it was on the video, almost lost in the
other noises. Somewhere, in between the sounds of
the crowd, and the noise of a bad PA system, a
distant siren screamed.

Of course, he'd noticed the sirens before when
he'd watched this video, and assumed they were for
Cadence. But the ambulance had already been

there, that day, the attendants already lifting her
onto the stretcher as the noise of the sirens grew.
They hadn't been answering the accident, they had
caused it. Storm was scared to death of the sound
of sirens.

He rubbed his aching head wearily. There was
more—he knew that. There had been no sirens on
other days when Storm was jumpy and hard to
handle. There were no sirens to explain his edginess
inside box stalls. But he had a suspicion, and he
knew he had to check it out. Because Cadence had
lost faith in the horse, and he had to convince her
the horse wasn't bad. Though if his reasoning was
correct . . . He frowned.

Maybe he didn't have to think about that just
yet. He had to check it out first, and protect the
horse from Cadence's wrath for a few days.

And maybe she needed a few days, too. A few
days away from the euphoric spell of her newfound
passion, and maybe she'd see him for what he was.
A cowpoke. With weather creases on his face, and
leather in his hide, and not much to offer a princess,
except a patch of earth and a handful of sky.

The next day he enlisted Sloan to check on the
horse for him and give a note to Cadence.

Sloan eyed him disapprovingly. "They used to
hang horse thieves."

"Just for a few days. That woman is capable of
doing grave harm when she's annoyed."

"Hmm. Sounds like the old princess to me. And
I don't want to tangle with her."

"Just give her the note, okay?"

"Ah, all right."

But, when it came time to go up to the house
and actually give her the note, Sloan couldn't find

it. He knew it must have slipped out of his shirt pocket while he was leaning over something or other, but he was disinclined to go and look for it. He did not handle women very well at the best of times. The thought of tangling with an angry one— and particulary when that angry one was Cadence Copperthorne—made finding that note a very low priority for him.

He had just about nicely managed to dismiss even the niggling little guilt from his mind when she stormed down to the barns.

He figured she looked fighting fit as he had ever seen her. It both pleased him and dismayed him.

"What did he do with my horse, Sloan?" she demanded.

Now Sloan was not a man accustomed to lying, but it seemed right now he was going to have to make a choice between her wrath or Dace's. And he could see Dace was quite right—she had murder on her mind. Besides, she wasn't nearly as scary as he knew Dace might be.

"I think the horse got left at the vet's," he said. "T'was hurt, you know."

For a minute dismay crossed her features, but only for a moment. "Not hurt as badly as it's going to be."

"He won't appreciate that, you know."

"What?" she asked, dangerously.

"Well, a man don't like that. A woman trying to protect him. A woman looking out for him. A woman trying to take care of all the little spills and right all the wrongs. He's got a hard head. That horse didn't hardly hurt him at all."

"The point is the horse is dangerous."

"Well, if that were the point, maybe you should have had him shot after *you* got hurt. It would hurt a man's pride that you could take your knocks, but you didn't want him to take his."

"Where's the horse, Sloan? And where's Dace?"

"Don't rightly know to either of them." He screwed up his courage. "Dace left an envelope for you before he left, but I cain't find it."

The anger fizzled and her face paled. Sloan thought she might faint.

"He's gone? Dace is gone?"

"I guess the note explained it all," he said awkwardly. He promised himself he'd look for it after all when he saw how distressed she was.

"I'm sure it probably did," she said quietly, her fire gone, all quiet composure now.

She turned and limped away, trying to hide the violent shaking of her shoulders.

Dace was gone. Oh, Lord, she'd known it. In the back of her heart she'd known it. He had seen. Yesterday he had seen how much she cared for him. How much she loved him. It had scared him away. Well, could she blame him?

She had been bitchy, strong-willed, and bad-tempered. No wonder he'd run. Dace Stanton had made it clear from the beginning that he thought her limp was the very least of her problems.

She had known anyway. Known it was too good to be true. In a way, she wondered if she hadn't been testing him yesterday. Saying, this is who I really am. Some good. Some bad, too. Some light, some darkness. Some laughter, some yelling. Some tenderness, some fire.

And he'd run. He was gone. She was glad Sloan couldn't find his note. She didn't want to read a note from him—some half-baked explanation as to why. He would try and take the sting out of it, if she knew Dace. Because there had always been an element of pity in what he'd felt for her. She knew that.

Nobody pities a wildcat.

Maybe nobody loved one, either. She knew it would be the most dreadful farce to be cared about for a role she played. And yet, for one more chance, she felt she could pretend to be docile and pleasant for the rest of her days.

No. That wasn't true. Well, he'd never promised her anything, anyway. He'd never said anything about tomorrow, or about the future. Dace Stanton had learned the tough way to stay in today. Too bad he'd never learned to stay.

CHAPTER TEN

DACE drove into the yard. It was late and he was tired. He glanced down at his watch—after eleven. He looked automatically toward Cade's window. The light burned, and he felt his heart begin to thud faster.

Hell, he had missed her. He hadn't known how much it was possible for a man to miss a woman, until he had spent this time away from her. And somewhere in those lonely days, and lonely miles, he had discovered a truth that was both frightening and exhilarating. He'd done something he'd promised himself he was never going to do. He'd fallen in love. For heaven's sake, he'd fallen in love with a she-devil.

And he'd learned something else. The deathly fear he felt of the pain that seemed to come part and parcel with relationships couldn't hold a candle to the pain he felt when he wasn't with her. It was rather humbling knowledge to have.

He gazed at her window, again, and frowned. When things had begun to get complicated, and he'd found himself in some godforsaken back-woods corner of blue-grass horse country, he'd called her to say it was going to take longer than he'd originally thought. She'd been out. He hadn't seen much point in leaving a message since there wasn't a number he could be reached at. He'd tried a couple more times. She was always out. Then he didn't leave a message because he was angry.

Out where? With whom? Lionel? Had he been ditched? Had she rediscovered her confidence in herself only to decide she had no more use for a cowboy? It was true that part of the reason he had left was to give her time to think about what she really wanted, but now he didn't feel as if he could bear it if what she really wanted didn't include him.

I could have Cadence back if I whistled. Funny, the things that could plague a man when he was lonely and tired.

Maybe she really had been that mad about him going to Storm instead of staying with her. Mad enough to go back to a man who was weaker... more easily controlled. Still, it couldn't be helped. That was part of his code of ethics, and if she didn't like it——

He wondered why he was arguing with her in his head, when he could have the pleasure of doing it in person. He thought about going to the door, but he didn't particularly want to get the whole house up—and he certainly didn't want the whole house to know he was in her room, because that would reduce the chances of her asking him to stay.

He did something he had always fantasized about doing. He began to climb the ivy trellis up to her room.

Cadence had not been out of her room in a week. She'd given instructions to Timothy that she was not to be disturbed in any circumstances. Then she had grieved. She'd cried. And fumed. And hit pillows and cursed, and shredded up the magazines that couldn't divert her attention from her heartache. She'd gone over their moments together and relived them, looking for clues to this ending.

And she'd thought she had found it. Right at the very beginning he had said to her, "When a man feels like up and walking away, you're best to just let him." It had probably been a warning. That he wouldn't stay. That there was no point in trying to make him stay. That there was no point in trying to capture that storm called love.

And it was his silly pride. She wished she'd explained herself better when it had come up. Explained to him that no, she didn't know how to cook, and had never done dishes, but dammit, she was no stranger to hard work, and she certainly was not afraid to learn new things or get her hands dirty.

Spoiled brat, he'd called at her. He might as well have added, You can't even do dishes.

But there had been no chance to explain. He had just gone without a farewell, and there was not much point in her torturing herself about the reasons. She'd rather hoped she would die, but she didn't. In fact, once or twice she had even found herself smiling when she thought of him. Now and then, she'd known the truth: she was not only going to live—she was going to be a better person for having been touched by the wonder of love.

Cadence froze, and quietly put down her plate of cookies. She had heard something outside. She threw back her covers and made her way over to the window, trying desperately to be quiet. Something was in the ivy outside her window. Fear hammered in her throat.

A cat, she told herself, trying to still the heavy beating of her heart so she could hear better.

If it was a cat, a more rational voice informed her, it must be a three-hundred-pound cougar for all the noise it was making.

Panic froze her ability to think. Finally, she shrank back against the curtains, groped around for her cane, and held it high over her head, waiting, ready.

With horror she watched as a credit card slipped in the window and the catch flipped up. The window squeaked open, and one long, denim-clad leg came in. She hit it, with all her might, with her cane.

There was a muffled curse, and then Dace catapulted through the window, and hopped around on one leg, obviously in great pain but trying to be quiet about it.

Cadence burst out laughing, but was quelled by the angry look he gave her.

"I told you what I was going to do to you if you ever used that cane as a weapon again," he hissed, gingerly testing some weight on his leg and then limping menacingly toward her.

She backed away from him, the cane held out aggressively in front of her. "I thought you were a criminal," she protested, and then felt a flare of real anger. "You are a criminal. Bloody horse thief! You were probably coming in here to get my wallet."

"Cadence," he said softly, threateningly, "put down the cane."

"I will not!"

"Would you keep your voice down?" he ordered quietly.

She sucked in a breath, planning to let out the longest, loudest shriek of her life. The bloody nerve of the man——

He leapt at her before the sound emerged. With one hand he took her cane and tossed it away; the other arm wrapped strongly around her, and pulled her toward him.

His mouth swooped down, and captured hers.

The scream died without much of a fight. She began to tremble and he picked her up and carried her across the room, dropped her on her bed and gazed down at her. Then he came down on top of her, and gave her the soundest kissing of her life.

"Dace," she whispered, "where have you been?"

"What do you mean, where have I been? I left you a note. Where have *you* been?"

"Sloan told me you'd left a note, but he couldn't find it...and I thought it probably just said goodbye...for good."

She saw pain flit through his eyes.

"It hurts me," he said softly, "that you think I could be so cruel."

She did not know how to tell him that her assumption was based on her own lack of confidence in her lovableness.

"So why did you go?" She reached up and touched the whisker-shadowed hollows of his cheeks, hoping her fingertips could tell him what pride prevented her lips from saying.

He kissed her fingertips. "Storm's mystery has been driving me crazy. I had to solve it once and for all. But never mind that, right now. Where have you been? Out gallivanting around the country, I guess?"

"Gallivanting? I've been locked in my room, licking my wounds. I told you, I thought you'd gone, Dace. I thought you'd gone for good. I thought you took one look at my wicked bad temper and headed for the hills.''

"You think I didn't have a clue before now that you have a temper? Lord, woman, you've been spitting and hissing and showing your claws since our first meeting.''

"I know," she said. "I'm horrible.''

"Horrible? Yes, you are. And adorable. You're a witch and an enchantress. You're a storm and you're the sunshine that follows. You're a woman. All woman. With every bit of the mystery and temperament that being a woman entails.

"Part of the reason I went was so you could figure out what you wanted. I know what I want. I love you. I've loved every single thing about you for a long, long time. And I plan to love it for a long time more, if you'll let me. I don't want a life that's dull and predictable, and I don't want a wife who's dull and predictable, either. I want you. High-spirited, and bad-tempered, and exciting. Like capturing a storm with all its magnificent energy and beauty and power. Living with you will be like riding a storm.''

"Wife?" she whispered incredulously.

"Can you think of one other good reason to climb up your trellis in the dead of night? Other than to propose to you?''

She laughed huskily. "Well, maybe one other.''

He smiled. "Hmm. I might have given that one a passing thought, too.''

"Scoundrel." She sobered. "I thought maybe you thought I was a spoiled, useless brat. I can learn to cook. I can do dishes. I can give away my money on street corners.''

Dace laughed. "When I left I really thought we had to solve all that stuff right away. Now I see that sharing a life with someone else is a process. We're always going to have things to resolve, and that will be a part of loving each other and learning from one another. We'll work out the details.

"Speaking of which," he said, lifting a stern eyebrow, "I hope this week of seclusion hasn't meant another week without seeing your doctor and your therapist."

"I keep telling you that's none of your business."

"And I keep telling you I'm making it my business."

"Okay," she conceded grouchily. "I went. And you needn't look so satisfied with yourself. I went because I knew it was time for me to take responsibility for my own health. I'm glad I did."

"Really? What's the charming blush all about?"

You couldn't put one single thing past Dace Stanton, she decided, bemused. "In those first few weeks after the accident I was in something of a daze. There was so much pain and disappointment to deal with that I just started shutting things out, not listening as closely as I could have.

"Some of the things…" her voice was somewhat choked "… that I thought I would never do normally, I will be able to do—with time and plenty of physio. For six months I had to restrict some of my movement—not for a lifetime. The therapist is going to start working on lateral movement again very soon."

"That's wonderful, Cadence." His eyes had the most wicked gleam in them, and she rushed on.

"I may even be able to ride again, some day. Oh, probably not competitively, but——" She stopped and stared at him. "What are you looking at me like that for?"

"Because you're her."

"Who?"

"The Cadence in the video. Even better, somehow. There's a depth mixed with the laughter in your eyes. Was it finding out you could ride again that did it, Cade? That gave you back something you'd been missing?"

Actually, she suspected her eyes had taken on that glow he was talking about in about the same instant that she'd recognized who her intruder was. But she didn't feel ready to let him know that, yet.

"Something's missing, all right, but I haven't got it back. Where's my horse?"

"He's safe from your bad temper."

"I wouldn't have really shot him."

"I know. Sold him, though?"

She laughed. "The advertisement is in the paper. Of course, I'm not answering the phone."

"Oh, baby, I'm so sorry you thought I'd leave you. I never wanted to cause you any more pain. It seems to me you've had enough." He sighed. "But I'm going to have to hurt you once more. What I found out about Storm isn't good."

She could see the agony in his eyes that the thought of hurting her caused him, and Storm didn't seem very important right now. "I don't think I would have ever known how much I loved you, Dace, if I hadn't had this week to miss you, to think about it. You just asked me to marry you, and that feels as if you gave me a suit of armor to wear against life's hurts. What can hurt me, when the man I love with all my heart and soul loves me back?"

"You're a brave and beautiful woman, Cadence," he said softly. "And tonight I'm going to lose myself in your bravery and your beauty and your special kind of magic. Enough time tomorrow to let the world back in."

He took her lips and gnawed gently on them, but the storm built in both of them as he went on to gently ravage her eyes and her nose and her cheeks and her neck. He dipped lower and she felt lightning bolts of thrilling tension rip through her. Her breath was coming in ragged gasps, and her heart was making thunder inside her.

Together, they rode the flashing heat of the storm into the unearthly still serenity that followed. She curled up in the strong circle of his arms. She had never felt so safe, so treasured, so cherished in all her life. She had found her shelter for all time.

A sharp rapping on the door woke her up. The first thing she felt was an odd tug of loss because she realized the bed beside her was empty.

"What?" She felt panicky. Had any of it been true? Or had it been the most delicious of dreams?

"Miss Cadence, *that* man is here again."

She giggled at Timothy's put-out tone. Somehow she didn't mind being called Cadence. At all. It was her name. And her spirit danced with the most astounding grace. Dace, she realized, had called her Cadence nearly from the beginning. Her name sounded so good and so right coming off his lips.

"Is he?" She noticed that this time it wasn't even morning. It wasn't even light out yet.

"Does he ever call at a normal hour? Does he ever call *normally*?" Timothy groused.

"Is he coming in?"

"No. He said he'd wait outside for you."

She made him wait, despite her own eagerness to be with him again. She showered, dressed meticulously in a calf-length white Indian cotton dress. She piled her abundance of red hair on top of her head and pinned it up, leaving soft tendrils to curl around her face. She draped a matching shawl of the beautiful cotton over the soft naked swell of her shoulders and went to meet Dace.

But when she first flung open the front door, she felt disappointed. She thought he would have the carriage. Instead, he sat astride Storm, looking down at her, a certain sadness in his face.

She stared up at him, feeling excluded—but only for a moment, because he reached down and caught her under her arms and swung her up, across his lap. He cradled her in his arms.

"Are you okay? Is that comfortable?"

She nodded. She had never felt as exquisitely feminine as she did in this moment.

He walked the horse out of sight of the house, and then broke into a trot.

"Still okay?" he asked her.

She nodded again, and he nudged the big horse into that smooth canter.

She began to cry. She had never thouht she would feel this again. The sheer joy of sitting on a horse, the wind stinging her face and tugging playfully at her hair. And some day she might do this again sitting astride her own horse. Maybe Dace would be racing at her side. Maybe children on fat ponies would be chasing them through sun-drenched meadows... She wept into Dace's chest.

He stopped on the crest of the hill, and his grip tightened on her. "The sun will come up over there," he said, nodding with his chin.

She could see a fine ribbon of light starting on the horizon and she fastened her eyes on it.

"I have to tell you the bad news now." He hesitated, tucked a piece of her wild red hair behind her ear. "He's been in a fire, Cadence. Storm was in a stable fire."

She didn't understand what he was trying to tell her.

"I tracked down his stable of origin using a bill of sale. He's changed hands a whole lot of times. Twelve, actually, before you bought him. I guess somewhere along the way the information about the fire wasn't passed on, and he just got labeled a problem horse."

"I don't understand what it means," she said, puzzled by the immense sadness in Dace's eyes as he looked down at her.

"Sirens," Dace said quietly. "The sound of a siren makes him go crazy. It must be as if the terror of that night is imprinted in him and certain things twig it. They always will, Cadence."

She stared at him.

"The smell of smoke. Sirens. Being kept inside. Those things are always going to terrify him. He's fourteen years old. I don't think he's going to change. I think it would be cruel to try and make him change, say by exposing him to sirens and smoke."

"What are you saying?"

He sighed. "Cadence, those are all things we couldn't control in a show situation. To a certain extent, we can control them out here, in the country, but at a show we can't control when a siren will go off, or when there's going to be smoke in the air.

You'll never get him to calm down inside a stable. Never."

"Dace——" The panic was rising in her voice. Just last night she had thought it didn't matter. But it did. She could not expect Dace to be her whole life. She would smother him. She had to have something else to direct her boundless energy at.

"I think the kindest thing you could do is retire him. We can ride him like this. For the pure pleasure of riding him. But he's never going to give you your gold, Cadence. I'm sorry."

"But what am I going to do?" she whispered brokenly into his chest. She cried. Gone. The dream was gone. There would never be another horse quite like this one. There would never be a feeling like the one he had given her. His immense spirit, his innate greatness, had made her feel so close, as if she could taste and touch and smell that gold medal. Now what?

"Cadence," he finally asked her softly, "isn't it obvious to you by now? What you should be doing? What you were probably born to do?"

"I thought I was born to win a gold medal," she croaked.

"And maybe you were. You have this incredible gift of being able to pass on what you know about your sport and about horses. There's a fire that burns in you, that ignites everything it touches. I don't know about gold medals, Cadence, but I know you should be using your gift. I know you should be teaching others how to get the most out of themselves. I know you've got a wicked eye for great horses, though I don't think I'll let you pick any more of your own pupils."

She stared at him wide eyed. Had it always been there, sparkling with such clarity, waiting for her to see it? His words gave her a peaceful sense of homecoming. She knew that he was right. That was exactly what she was supposed to do: choose great horses and coach great riders.

"Aren't you going to be one of my pupils any more, Dace?"

He shook his head, and looked deep into her eyes. "No, ma'am. I like jumping horses. In open fields, with the wind in my face and the silence all around me. There's a freedom about it—an illusion of joining eagles."

She felt a small twist of sadness but somehow she had known all along that, though a man with such monumental self-assurance could fit in anywhere, there were only a few places he would call home. In her heart she had known the show arena was not one of them.

She managed to smile. "Somehow I think Storm will like it much better, too. I want you to have him. The two of you belong together."

Dace laughed. "No, the two of *us* belong together. But Storm is a very special animal, and he has a place in my heart. I'll accept on the condition that it will be the last extravagant gift from you."

"Maybe some day yet I'll present you with a gold medal," she promised him.

"I was riding for the gold, too," Dace informed her softly. "But I got the gold I was riding for."

"Did you?" she asked with surprise.

"I was riding for the gold of your eyes, Cadence. I wanted to see them the way they looked in those videos. Full of laughter and life and contentment. Full of fire and spirit—putting every other kind of gold on this earth to shame. I was riding for the gold. And I got it. In some ways, I got so much more than I started out for. Because now there is a wisdom and pain tempering the gold of your eyes that makes you beautiful beyond mere physical beauty.''

She started to cry again, this time with joy mingled with her sadness.

''It seems to me I put a dream on hold,'' he continued, stroking her hair, ''and it's time to get back to it. I've got enough money saved to get the Charolais bull I like; to build a house on my land. And I've got enough maturity, now, to know that I have to balance work—that I don't have to prove to anyone that I'm a man by working myself to death. And I have enough courage, now, to love. To love you with everything I've got, for the rest of my days.''

They were silent for a long time, and then he nudged her. ''Look.''

And she looked and saw dawn spreading its golden fingers across the land. The show was spectacular, the whole world painted for a moment in the brilliant, golden light of hope, of new beginnings, of dawn.

''You see,'' he said quietly. ''There are so many different kinds of gold that are worth having.'' He nodded over the gold-drenched landscape. ''This one only seems free. It's not. It takes a lot of heartache before a man looks at this and understands the value of it. It's a gold worth riding for, too, Cadence.''

She nodded against him, feeling a languid sense of having enough. Right now. In this moment. Her tears had left her exhausted and at peace, too. Yes, there would be other kinds of gold worth having, worth striving toward.

Dace cleared his throat. "There's this kind of gold, too." He pressed a piece of crinkly tissue paper into her hand.

She leaned against him, and opened it carefully. Folded tenderly within it was a beautiful, simple, solid gold wedding band.

"It was my mother's," he said, a growl of emotion in his voice.

"Oh, Dace, it's beautiful." The gold was mellow, shining a soft liquid yellow that put the sun to shame.

"I can't promise you gold medals. And maids are out of the question. But this——" he swept his hand over the lingering gold of the morning landscape "—I can promise you this."

And then she knew. Her obsession with gold was a small and petty thing in comparison to what she felt for this man who wanted so much for her to have her dreams, for her to know the joy of contentment, the simple peace of being loved.

It was time, now, to put away the dreams of a little girl, and to begin to dream the dreams of a woman. Dreams spun of gold—and lace. Dreams of bassinets and big brass beds. Dreams of loving and being loved.

She knew at last she had found real gold. It wasn't out there somewhere, but it was that thing that shone endlessly inside her. Love. Love was forever gold.

Dace looked at her face, and had to bite his lip against the sweet agony the light that glowed there caused in him. He gathered her tight against him, and spurred toward the gold ball of the rising sun.

HARLEQUIN ROMANCE®

**Harlequin Romance
knows that lasting love
is something special...**

And so is
next month's
title in

THE BRIDAL COLLECTION

TEMPORARY ARRANGEMENT
by Shannon Waverly

THE BRIDE was an unwelcome guest.
THE GROOM was a reluctant host.
The arrangement was *supposed*
to be temporary but—
THE WEDDING made it for keeps!

Available this month in
The Bridal Collection
RESCUED BY LOVE
by Anne Marie Duquette #3253

WED12

Following the success of WITH THIS RING and
TO HAVE AND TO HOLD, Harlequin brings you

JUST MARRIED

SANDRA CANFIELD
MURIEL JENSEN
ELISE TITLE
REBECCA WINTERS

just in time for the 1993 wedding season!

Written by four of Harlequin's most popular authors, this
four-story collection celebrates the joy, excitement and
adjustment that comes with being "just married."

You won't want to miss this spring tradition, whether
you're just married or not!

**AVAILABLE IN APRIL WHEREVER HARLEQUIN
BOOKS ARE SOLD**

HARLEQUIN 🦘 PRESENTS®

A Year
DOWN UNDER

In 1993, Harlequin Presents celebrates the land down
under. In April, let us take you to Queensland, Australia,
in A DANGEROUS LOVER by Lindsay Armstrong,
Harlequin Presents #1546.

Verity Wood usually manages her temperamental boss,
Brad Morris, with a fair amount of success. At least she
had until Brad decides to change the rules of their
relationship. But Verity's a widow with a small child—the
last thing she needs, or wants, is a dangerous lover!

Share the adventure—and the romance—
of A Year Down Under!

Available this month in
A YEAR DOWN UNDER

THE GOLDEN MASK
by Robyn Donald
Harlequin Presents #1537
Wherever Harlequin books are sold.

Where do you find hot Texas nights, smooth Texas charm and dangerously sexy cowboys?

COWBOYS AND CABERNET

Raise a glass—Texas style!

Tyler McKinney is out to prove a Texas ranch is the perfect place for a vineyard. Vintner Ruth Holden thinks Tyler is too stubborn, too impatient, too... Texas. And far too difficult to resist!

CRYSTAL CREEK reverberates with the exciting rhythm of Texas. Each story features the rugged individuals who live and love in the Lone Star State. And each one ends with the same invitation...

Y'ALL COME BACK...REAL SOON!

Don't miss **COWBOYS AND CABERNET** by Margot Dalton. Available in April wherever Harlequin books are sold.

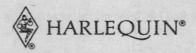 HARLEQUIN®

THE TAGGARTS OF TEXAS!

Harlequin's Ruth Jean Dale brings you
THE TAGGARTS OF TEXAS!

Those Taggart men—strong, sexy and hard to resist...

You've met Jesse James Taggart in FIREWORKS!
Harlequin Romance #3205 (July 1992)

And Trey Smith—he's THE RED-BLOODED YANKEE!
Harlequin Temptation #413 (October 1992)

And the unforgettable Daniel Boone Taggart in SHOWDOWN!
Harlequin Romance #3242 (January 1993)

**Now meet Boone Smith and the Taggarts who started it all—
in LEGEND!
Harlequin Historical #168 (April 1993)**

Read all the Taggart romances!
Meet all the Taggart men!

Available wherever Harlequin Books are sold.